DRES

CAROLYN SLAUGHTER

Dresden, Tennessee

faber and faber

First published in 2007
by Faber and Faber Limited
3 Queen Square London WC1N 3AU

Typeset by Faber and Faber Limited
Printed in England by Mackays of Chatham, plc

A CIP record for this book
is available from the British Library

ISBN 987-0-571-23143-0
ISBN 0-571-23143-8

2 4 6 8 10 9 7 5 3 1

For Thomas Moore
with love and gratitude

DRESDEN, TENNESSEE

Kurt slept with a sheet over his face and occasionally it would wrap itself around his neck, as it had this morning, but, for a moment there, when he was under, there'd been a sense of suffocation. He held onto the dream: the bomber plane had left a hum in his brain that seemed to have risen to the ceiling, vibrating there. He was ten again, running across the lawn, carrying high above his head a model aeroplane, one of his father's RAF bombers from World War II: a Lancaster, massive, dark-bellied, heavy, and load-ed with bombs. The model aeroplane became real and he was flying it and watching it at the same time. He could just make out the roundels on the wings and a leather-helmet-ed face at the window wearing dark goggles. He was flying fast, as if the dream were shot on speeded-up film, black and white, real as that. Now he was the gunner, perched in the icy cockpit at the rear, waiting for the marked red target to become clear and for the flares to disperse into the dark-ness. The Lancaster was circling through the air, orbiting, and then it dropped below the clouds and there was only the night sky and the city, undefended, belly up. He dipped his arm, adrenaline pumping through his brain as he wait-ed for the drop, feeling the purest exhilaration as he whis-pered: clear cloud, check position and signal, get clear, approach target, hold it. NOW. He threw back his head and yelled: Bombs away! Master bomber! Carnage! Total anni-hilation! FIRE! The lawn fried, turning black in an instant.

At the window, his father stood, watching him, not moving.

The clock with its soft detonating tick announced that it was five on the nail. He pulled up the covers, his hand moving companionably down his groin and resting a moment on the shaft of his penis. For a second when he'd woken, he hadn't been sure where he was: which hotel or what day. Lately, he'd become aware of a change in direction, a movement away from the Lower East Side; now he was circling mid-town and keeping close to the railway stations. His jeans were flung over his black coat, a Gap shirt, pale blue, a white tee-shirt and his square, wide, brown leather bag, old and battered, sturdy as hell, given him when he'd graduated, and now one of the last connections to the old life. Lying on his side in his own warmth, he imagined other bodies in other beds: a man running his hand over the smooth slope of a woman's hip and belly; a child turning in its cot, a lone man jerked out of sleep by the imperative of an alarm, a couple coiled together, the man lost in the woman's hair. As he thought of getting up, he imagined a man sitting on the edge of a rumpled bed, checking the night calls on his cell; a woman in a blue nightgown filing her nails, a child solitary at a kitchen table, stuffing Cheerios into his mouth. In Germany, it was the middle of the morning: 11.07 to be precise.

On the street outside his window, he listened to the first shuffle of morning: early commuters headed for the station across the way or waiting for the bus; coffee putt-putting on black discs in the deli, bacon frying, a brown bag of bagels tipped on its side; the sounds of trucks slowing to slap newspapers down on sidewalks close to the kiosks; the windy sound of bus brakes, the early morning

2

quiet of a city about to explode into life. He thought of the people out there, reluctantly taking up their daily business, going to the same cramped cell in a line of partitioned space or a mahogany desk overlooking Park Avenue, piles of paperwork, song of the laptops. It seemed so far away, fluttering briefly behind his eyes before sinking, but for a second he envied them. Especially those who were married with children, who came to the city to work, but whose real life went on in a gardened suburb, with its tedious and lovely predictability of departure and return: the same rooms with their accumulations of memory and time, the fortress of home.

On the street, a woman was staring up at the sky, and then her hands flew to her mouth as her eyes widened, and a man in a dark coat dropped his *New York Times* and began running wildly in the opposite direction, his coattails flapping behind him like a cartoon character. And there were others whose lives were moving in the same sweet rhythm as always, oblivious. Kurt decided that he'd get out of bed at precisely 5.55. He liked the conformity of the three figures, and five was a lucky number, like three and seven. Numbers were pleasing to him, calming in the days when he'd been some kind of number-cruncher, knew how to make things add up. The certainty of numbers, like the consolation of music, didn't change when other things did. And he'd always been able to remember numbers – how much he had in his accounts at any time – dates, phone numbers, that kind of thing. The small black electric clock calmed him; its regular tick had a familiarity that was becoming vital. No need to set the alarm; the numbers were set in his brain and would wake him when it was time. He dozed lightly and, between the shifting layers of sleep and half-sleep, a woman's face, just for an

3

instant, rose out of the pool of memory: round cheeks, a sprinkle of pale freckles on the upper slopes of her cheek-bones, a mouth plump and finely etched. He shuffled around for a name without locating one, closing his eyes to recapture the face, but it had gone. The sun was coming up, a flare between two heavy damask curtains, cutting across the carpet like a yellow marker. The cleaners were about and, since he always took a room on the ground floor, as close to the exit as possible, the gathering roar of vacuum cleaners merged with the drone of approaching taxis and the sirens in the distance.

For a full fifteen minutes, he allowed himself to become submerged in sleep again. Until, there was no question about it, the walls were shaking, even as outside the cars were now whipping by fast and furious, no lull, no let-up. He flung his feet out of bed and onto the floor. He was dressed and zipping up the bag when he felt the rocking under his feet, and froze. How late was it? For a moment he saw an explosion of images and snapped his eyes shut to try to block them out: a mother carrying a wicker clothes-basket and taking a child's hand down from the branches of the apple tree, kneeling to pick up four pieces of her oldest son, a bit of his face with his black curls blown off, an ear with a gold stud, a tooth, a piece of his red-checked shirt with his intestines in it. The lower leg of her youngest son was floating in the stream; she knew it by the scar on his ankle where he'd fallen from his tricycle onto a piece of glass. She lifted the smooth, small limb out of the water, dried it on her dress and kissed it, placing it in the basket on top of the other body parts, neatly, the way she folded laundry.

From the time he'd first read the article, he'd been trying to erase the images and now, shaking with a sorrow he couldn't contemplate, he wondered, Was it Them, or was it Us? Weren't we the same? Who was doing what? And why this place, not even a night strike, and only a small target? Why this place except how little it takes to bring a city to its knees. He was running down the hallway to the lobby, clutching his bag to his chest. The grey-suited receptionist, eyes sleepy and dull, glanced up from her computer and smiled at him, then backed off as he rushed towards her. He was sweating as he dropped his bag, reached across the desk and gripped her arm: Sound the main alarm. Get everyone out of here. Do it now. He shook her hard. NOW. He picked up his bag and ran for the revolving door, but it moved in such a ponderous way that he threw his whole weight against the glass to try to speed it up and, in the helplessness of the moment, he was enraged again.

Outside in the cold February air, his body came to attention and he slowed down. He began to count his steps, walking without haste, his bag no longer clutched to his chest but in his right hand, as usual. No one looked at him and he kept his eyes straight ahead like a soldier, merging with the rising flood of people heading for the transportation systems. The sky was white, the faintest pink on the far horizon. He heard a bird, and another. The trees were leafless and grey. A commotion was starting up on the street: two women were looking up at the windows of his hotel, frowning, talking to one another, heads butting together in agitation. Then they moved on, looking back, walking faster, not looking back, holding hands, running. The man selling papers put down his cup of coffee and sniffed the air. Twice he had to be asked for a copy of the *Wall Street Journal*, but by then a stream of people had their hands and dollars reaching out towards him and he forgot the smell. A small girl being taken to school, tugged at her nanny's coat and pointed – Look! Look! – but they were late and the nanny pulled her along faster.

Kurt was cutting across, dodging traffic, joining the swarm headed for Penn station. He entered on the 8th Avenue side, but just before he pushed through the door, he hesitated. He didn't turn back to look, but seemed to be waiting for something to happen. All quiet. As he walked down to the bottom, he was counting the stairs, then stopped counting and walked swiftly through the crowd to the main concourse where, looking up at the train departure times, he made a quick decision and joined the queue to the ticket office. He was sweating profusely. He took off his coat and checked his watch. A man standing beside him started to complain about the price of the Amtrak tickets. Kurt nodded, turning his head away. It was what he did now to avoid questions. He was thinking about Mississippi and Tennessee, the names on the guidebooks in his bag, and how much he liked the double 's's, the way they held together, making a unit. He was going South. It was a compulsion, something instinctive that pulled him out of the city. He'd first felt the urgency in Barnes & Noble when he'd been strolling through the travel book section and the two names jumped out at him, even though neither place meant anything to him. He'd take a train to Newark and then fly to Memphis, perhaps, it would depend on the planes. But where would you find the South, really, was it a place lost and forgotten or was it still possible to find the aftershocks of those pictures that swam up of dogs straining at leashes and people with straight backs ignoring the taunts, walking to school?

A man and a woman were running across the main concourse to the trains on the east-side platforms. They were covered in grey dust and were almost barging into people

as they ran. Someone yelled, Hey, asshole, what's the fucking rush? The man was running as if on a football field;
he'd left the woman far behind and wasn't even looking
back to see if she was still following him. Kurt panicked
for a moment and looked for the nearest exit, but since he
was next up, he moved forward and leaned into the glass
square of the booth. He wished he could take an Amtrak,
but it was too late. He didn't want to take the New Jersey
Transit train; it meant going into the herd gathering at the
stairs to Platform 13E, but there was no choice now. He got
his ticket and headed for his platform, hoping he wouldn't
see the couple again. He had less than five minutes to get
on the train and out the station. Checking his watch again,
he was terrified that he was going to hear over the inter-
com an order to evacuate the station, and after he'd run
down the stairs he stood on the platform for a second, listening, but he heard nothing. All clear.

At Newark, he bought a first-class ticket on the first
plane going South; the one to Birmingham was leaving in
an hour and the one to Charlotte had already left, so he
booked a flight to Memphis. On the plane he took his seat;
he'd insisted on one close to the exit, in case, but the seat
he'd wanted was taken. The economy and business sec-
tions of the plane had filled up, but first class was almost
empty: there were two business men at the back, and a
woman in a fur coat with a small baby. He could see the
baby, it was about four months old and he didn't know
why he knew that. Its face was very still, slightly blue-
looking in the light. A woman who was well dressed and
sharp-looking had just come in and was sitting down in
the seat nearest the door. It was where he'd wanted to sit,
and he'd intended, after take-off, to make the switch. For a
moment, he wondered if he should move, but then he'd be

7

further back and anyway it was too late now because she, lifting her face from a black-bound document on her lap, smiled at him and he saw that her face was a little freckled and her curly hair was threaded with red and copper, and nice. He smiled back and then for some reason asked her how long it would take to fly to Memphis. Two and a half hours, she said, something like that, though it takes longer than it should. He couldn't resist asking, Why's that? She shrugged and laughed. It should take less than that to get from New York to Memphis. Kurt said, It's 956 miles. She looked at him with amusement: That's something I'd never notice – how far from one place to the next. She looked down and sipped her coffee and he wished he'd been less agitated and got one himself, and then he wanted a cigarette, rather urgently, though as far as he knew, he didn't smoke. As she crossed her legs, there was a slight rustling sound and he was aroused by it. It was the weird thing about sex, he thought, what triggered desire, the sound, like leaves blown against the limbs of a tree.

The woman was moving through the pages of the document, she was a quick reader, or a skimmer, hard to say. Watching her, he remembered her eyes: hazel, with finely traced eyebrows, manicured, he thought, liking the grooming, the charcoal skirt and jacket, the high boots, the new, shiny briefcase, so unlike his own. She put the document aside and looked out the window. As she put her left hand on the seat, he noticed it was ring-less and, though she'd moved away a bit, she somehow seemed nearer. And then for a split second, like a hallucination, he saw a thin gold band on her wedding finger. The plane was picking up speed, and the engine seemed suddenly very loud, as if it occupied the entire space of his brain. He felt heavy. As the plane lifted into the clouds, his sense of relief about leaving the city was so great that it felt like pure joy – so much so that he turned to the woman and impulsively blurted out: Back there, when we left New York, I thought Penn station was gonna blow.

✑ 2 ✑

You're kidding? She spun round to face him, knees lined
up, and for a moment he remembered how, before catching his train to Newark, he'd seen a flustered, running couple who were covered in ash. It had been disturbing, that
sense of panic and fear, that déjà vu.

Did you see a couple, he asked her, at Penn Station, covered in ash?

I saw a man running, she said, looking kinda out of it
and dusty, and it threw me a bit, the associations, I guess.
Why d'you ask? She looked at Kurt expectantly, but he
wasn't responding to her and she waited for a while before
she asked, You a cop or something? FBI? He laughed, Hell
no. He was looking closely into her eyes, wondering what
might have given her that impression. She glanced at the
book he was reading, there was an umlaut above the 'u' in
Gunter and a picture of an old ship drowning in black seas,
and she looked at him as if she wanted to ask him something, but changed her mind.

I think, he said, there may have been something going
on in the city this morning.

Like what?

I saw smoke coming from a hotel, but it was probably
just a fire rather than a terrorist attack. It's so easy to ter-
rorize a city, a whole country: you don't need much – just
a bar on Second Avenue, a hotel near a railway station.
He'd alarmed her, he could tell; she looked at him suspi-
ciously and for one crazy moment he wondered if she

thought he was an Islamic extremist or a Palestinian or an Israeli or some lunatic from the woods of Arkansas.

I'm not sure, she said cautiously, what you're talking about. What hotel near what railway station?

It's easy, he said quickly, to become paranoid these days. She nodded. Sure is. She leaned across for a moment, not to actually go over, just to shake hands: I'm Hannah Brown, she said. He got up. My name's Kurt Altman. He said it in a polite, almost formal way. She waited a moment and then asked, You German? She smiled. First or second generation? For a moment he hesitated. Yes, he said, I'm German. He looked away. I was born here, but my parents were born there. It's funny, when you asked, I didn't want to admit it, being German, I mean. He grinned, You know, once a German, always a German. He shifted until his back faced the window. Not that I've ever been there. Well, perhaps, as a baby. I'm not sure. She frowned: Your parents didn't tell you whether you'd ever been to Germany?

No. He leaned forward and smiled. Your name, he asked, is it English?

Now it is.

It was Braun, like Eva? Right?

Eva wasn't Jewish, she said defensively.

And you are.

Some.

I thought you might be, he said.

We must have recognized each other.

I'm not Jewish, he said.

She closed her eyes. Oh boy, she whispered.

He smiled. It's not a big deal.

And then she moved back from him. He retreated too, but he didn't open the book and she didn't return to the document. She kept her eyes closed. He was wondering what kind of men she liked, what kind of lovers she'd had. He thought she was attracted to him, but he couldn't be sure. His eyes travelled from the coils of her hair across the slope of her forehead to her mouth and throat. He was mesmerized by the slow rise and fall of her breasts.

What d'you do? His voice was low and easy and he was looking at the document on her lap; it partially covered her knee but her thigh shimmered where the skirt had risen up; he could just detect a small cut on her skin, from a razor or the claw of a cat. His heart contracted for a moment.

I'm a communication consultant, she said, angling her body back in his direction. I work with corporations just after they've emerged from a financial mess – bankruptcy, an accounting scandal, insider trading – that kind of thing. She stopped, but he was still looking at her. He'd abolished the distance they'd just created, sitting closer to her, but not too close, the aisle a kind of no-man's-land between them. Well, she said, my job's to look at what's led to the fraud or the revenue-accounting improprieties – I talk to the fat cats, whose giant bonuses and gross-ups have landed them in court or jail – and then I talk to everyone around them who were part of the deception. She smiled a little ruefully: I teach people how to detect lies, how not to be lied to, and also how to rat on their boss without getting fired, but in ways different from the measures put out by the Sarbanes-Oxley Act.

As he listened to her he could see tall windows in an office that seemed familiar, and for a moment he heard some words, about a transaction that involved twenty-eight million dollars, and that was it. He looked quickly across at her. How long you been doing this?

Five years.

Must be stressful.

Actually, she said, it's kind of exciting. Sometimes I get lucky and I can get in when someone's just begun to unearth a fraud and has the guts to report it. That's pretty cool.

Always start at the top?

Those guys seldom carry the can.

D'you work with the scapegoats – personally, I mean?

No, but we refer them to people who do.

He smiled gingerly, You keep away from the personal suffering?

She smiled back, I guess.

It's your own company?

I have a partner. She and I do seminars – preventative stuff – the boards are interested in that. That's what I'm doing in Memphis. I wanted to get away from New York where the frauds are so massive. She looked at him and then away, shoving her hair back so her skin seemed pale and vulnerable. Tough kind of work, he said thoughtfully. She nodded. Miriam, my partner, she likes the really big deals, but I've been feeling overwhelmed by the sheer volume of the billions, and by this nauseating way CEOs have of pretending to be retards. His pulse quickened and he felt a strange buzz in his brain; it was like he was following her across a field planted with landmines.

Lately, though, she said, some interesting things have been happening in the South and it sort of drew me back.

You're from there? You don't have an accent.

There was a silence in which she seemed to be thinking hard. He noticed that she was looking intently at him, focusing not on his eyes, but his mouth, and he thought she was running some kind of check.

What, he asked, in your life, prepared you for this kind of work?

13

For the first time, she gave him her full attention. I come, she said, from a world of men with pick-up trucks and dead deer in the back – a far cry from corporate city . . .

I was wondering more about the lies, he said.

My lies?

Sure. Tell me about your lies.

She turned her body to face him, put the document on the seat and adjusted her skirt to cover her knees. Well, here's the main one, she said. My mother's Jewish, so's my father, but some years ago his business in Atlanta tanked, he went nuts, and after that we weren't Jewish any more. He became a born-again Christian, forced my mom to be the same and bought a farm in Louisiana. Dragged us all down there, hadn't a clue what he was doing. My mother held things together, got a job working with a group of attorneys in Jackson. My brothers lost the plot, dropped out of school, started growing weed out back and selling stolen cars – usual thing. I got out of Tallulah as if there was a fire behind me . . .

Beautiful name, he said.

Tallulah? Armpit of a place. I fled to New York. I was eighteen. It was '92. I'd managed to get into NYU, picked up a couple of psych and communication degrees, met a smart cookie called Miriam. She and I started the company and we were off to the races. There's no shortage of business and most years we can pretty much double it. She breathed out. And that's it. She looked him in the eye: What about you?

He smiled. How will you know if I'm lying?

I'll know.

How can you tell?

Body movement, eyes, use of language, tone, insistence, repetition. You realize, I'm sure, she said, her voice sliding,

14

becoming Southern, how avoidant you're being?

I'm just wondering what happens with memory and lies . . .

Meaning?

Is memory a lie, since it can never be really accurate?

I don't think so: words are slippery, but if there's no intent to lie . . .

But what if the memories are fragmented?

All memory is fragmented, but it doesn't make it untrue. Lying is reinventing, usually for some gain. The folks I work with use lies to get out of trouble while getting someone else into it.

She was looking steadily at him, waiting for him to tell her what he did. I was in business, he said reluctantly. Made a lot of money when everyone else was cleaning up, but we didn't get trashed to the same degree when the happy hour was over. His voice was glib. He wanted to leave it at that, but knew she wasn't going to let him. Recently, he said, I started to hate it all, dealing with money, the rush of dealing, even being pleasant to people, it all became a strain. He looked directly at her for the first time. One day I just couldn't go in to work. His voice deepened. I didn't answer the calls or emails and then I moved out of my apartment. For a while I spent my days drifting around the city, walking for hours, just wandering with no purpose . . .

How long did you do this?

Three weeks or so.

Where did you sleep?

Hotels.

No plan?

Nope. He put his hand to his head and saw her face shift from curiosity to concern. He forced himself to keep talking, but this was the last thing he needed, particularly from someone like her.

Go on, she said quietly.

He braced himself. And then one day, he said, I was talking to an anthropologist in a bar – and this guy, he was at Princeton – he started talking about violence, needing to see it up close in his line of work. Kurt was on safe ground again and his voice reflected it. He'd just come back from Africa, he said, was doing a PhD in violence, the ethnic kind, and then he was going on about the South, moving back and forth between genocide and slavery. Anyway, I couldn't get his ideas out of my brain. And I realized I'd lived in New York City all my life and never really seen much of the country, or even thought about it – how it really works in the South for example – the repercussions of slavery, the aftershocks of the Civil War – how those events gut the places where they happened. I sort of felt ashamed. This guy in the bar was talking about the impact of war and genocide on generations and how, without records, there isn't going to be a way for people to know the history so they can understand why they're the way they are. His face cleared. I hadn't realized till this minute how that conversation led me to buy a ticket south to Memphis.

And you wanted to know, suddenly, like that, about the South? Why?

He shrugged. I'd like to say something slick, but I think, on this trip, you and me, perhaps I'll abide by your disciplines and say I can't tell you what happened. I just felt a compulsion to go south the same way I had to get out of the corporate world. One day something snapped and I left my life behind me, or it left me. I can't tell you how or why, but everything changed. And I had to keep moving. That was the essential thing: to walk, to keep moving. She

16

waited. But he wasn't going to talk any more. His mouth closed in two lines, making a total. After a while, they were offered a drink and that broke the tension a bit. I felt, he said, without looking at her, a little crazy at times: no job to go to, none of the buddies around, no routine. I thought of guys who get axed who go to work every day, putting on the suit, kissing the wife goodbye in the morning and catching the train to spend the entire day in the park or bar before riding the 6.02 back home. And for a while it's great because the severance is coming in and no one knows about it and then after six months he goes to the bottom of the yard and shoots himself in the head.

He looked out the window. It's hard to think back, he said, almost as if there's nothing there. He turned to her and asked, What are you thinking? Right now? This minute?

She looked startled for a moment, but answered immediately. I was wondering if you were another of those lying bastards who've consumed, single-handedly, the entire life savings of a company's investors.

He laughed, hard, and with such enthusiasm that she couldn't help but do the same. She turned her body towards his. When was all this? When you left your job and apartment?

About a month ago, he said. Maybe more, maybe less. He looked at her, I walk for hours and hours, for whole days, as if I'm looking for something, but I don't know what. In the day time it's okay, but at night the sounds are so loud, the lights bother me, and there's a strange smell, like smoke, and it can be overwhelming. I seem to end up in places where things are burning, where homeless people are making fires in the rubble of a demolished building, and ghetto kids are setting fire to cars. When I feel a bit

17

too out-there, I head back to mid-town and find a hotel. He couldn't quite believe he was telling her all this, but she listened without shock or disbelief. When she spoke her voice was quiet. It sounds awful, she said. He smiled as if it weren't. She looked at him. What was your personal life like a month ago? Her eyes drifted to his left hand. There's a slight indentation, she said, on your finger, as if you were or are married. Did something happen?

He glanced at his left hand, and then back at her without speaking. He was disorientated, out of time, jolted back into a segment of the past where all he could see was a woman's face, crying, and a sound that went thud, thud, thud. They were given their ginger ales and he drank half of his before putting down his glass with a clunk.

I don't remember, he said.

∽ 3 ∽

He'd annoyed her. He could tell by the way her foot tapped in short bursts, as if she wanted to kick something, but the odd thing was in spite of her annoyance he wanted to get up and kiss her. When, a little later, he leaned across into her territory, he met a cool stare. He pulled himself out of the spaceyness he'd fallen into with her question about marriage and rings. I had an accident. Nothing serious, but it's left me with some memory loss . . . so when I told you I didn't know. I was trying to be truthful.

I'm sorry, she said, I thought you were jerking me around. What happened?

I walked into a plate-glass door, he said quickly, I was tired, not thinking straight. I whacked my head – got some kind of concussion. I was told it wouldn't last, but everything's been shifted around by the blow. Sometimes I feel a mild confusion about time. My memory's clear on the immediate past – going back a month or so – but blanked out, mostly, about all the rest. He looked at her with a wry grin. It's kinda terrifying.

She nodded and was quiet for a while. If you were married, or divorced, wouldn't you know that from your daily life?

There isn't any daily life, or none that relates to anything in the past. His breathing was shallow and he was getting hot. I think I'm divorced, he said quickly, I know it on some level, but it also doesn't feel particularly real to me. His voice hardened. No one can explain any of this, or give me a diagnosis, so it's hard to get a grip on it. Her face looked concerned and it was too much for him. He didn't want any more questions.

Why, she said quietly, didn't you say before that you were divorced? You said you didn't remember. She spoke in a way that was impersonal, and part of him appreciated the neutrality while the other half felt like he'd become one of the liars and thieves being skewered in one of her post-bankruptcy interrogations.

To say I didn't remember was true, he said quietly, or as much like the truth as I can pull up right now. It's difficult to admit your memory's up the creek.

Sure. It must be scary and disorientating. But – she smiled – you aren't responsible for what you don't remember.

Aren't I? Confusion began to gather with an intensity that created a roaring in his head. He tried to compose himself, but just at that moment the plane ploughed into some heavy turbulence, engines struggling against high winds. He was panicking. He tried to talk himself down: nothing to worry about, it would pass, just breathe. The sun shone directly into his eyes and he shut them quickly. The pilot's voice came on with a soft crackle, asking passengers to put on their seat belts. The crossed-out cigarette and buckle signs lit up on the console above his head. He put his feet together, straightened his back, and in a few minutes, as the plane began to stabilize, the clouds drifted back into view, obliterating the sun and the blue, and for a moment, no more than that, he was walking with his mother down a dusty street in some country place, who knows where, but it was calming, the way the two of them walked together, his mother holding his hand and swinging it occasionally, and once she lifted it to her lips and kissed his fingers. She was wearing a blue linen dress, kind of 80s in style, and her hair was reddish-brown and curly and he knew her name was Elsa Altman, who was married to Wilhelm Altman. Retrieving his parents' names was like hauling a huge salmon out of deep, swiftly running water.

He could breathe again; he repeated the names, the way, sometimes, looking at his driver's licence in his wallet, he tried out his own name, Kurt Altman, to see if the name fitted the face he no longer recognized in the mirror. And there'd been another shift: Altmann now had two 'n's – just like Tennessee. He smiled. Something settled. It was quiet, this memory, and he wanted to stay with his mother, but the image was breaking up. After a while another image moved in: his mother in a garden with trees that didn't grow in the north and flowering plants he couldn't find names for. She was pouring lemonade and they were waiting for someone whose name was Trudi. His mother was very calm . . . he felt as if he were falling asleep . . . and suddenly there was an explosion at the back of the plane . . . his head rammed against the seat, and for a split second he saw a stream of white light, like a flare, momentary, brilliant, gone.

The pilot landed so heavily it felt like the belly of the plane had crashed on the runway; it juddered, and with a slow shrieking began to veer about. He could smell burning. The passengers sat with white knuckles gripping the arms of their seats. The plane raced and rocked. His ears were popping and it was hard to breathe. The baby across the way was asleep and the stillness of the child disturbed him. He wondered if the plane was over its weight capacity and would blow any minute. They overstuffed aircraft these days, all those strikes, and the fuel shortage, and he'd read somewhere that a plane had taken off with one engine down and the pilot had carried on anyway. There was a crash and instinctively he doubled up in his seat and put his arms over his head. In a second Hannah had unbuckled her seat belt and crossed over. You okay? He straightened up. She sat down and fastened her seatbelt. As the plane stopped rocking and began to taxi down the runway, they both breathed again. That was rough, she said. Sure you're okay? She put her hand on his arm. Is it your head? No, he said, it's not my head. The pilot's voice came on again, apologizing, but giving no reason for bringing the plane down that way. The all-clear came and the passengers were like refugees on a freight train, shoving and stampeding. The pilot's voice came back, ordering everyone to resume their seats.

As soon as he could, he stood up, pulled down Hannah's overnight bag and handed it to her, and moved back to his side to get his own. She spoke from behind him. Where are you staying in Memphis? He turned round, I'm not sure. She opened her eyes wide and looked at him with a puzzled smile. Memphis, he said, was the first flight available. It seemed as good a place as any. It occurred to him that Memphis was the name of an ancient Egyptian city and, as they were waiting to disembark, he asked her if it was where Martin Luther King was assassinated. She nodded – On the balcony of his room at the Lorraine Motel. The cover of a Middle School History book appeared for a moment, and then the face of the man, clear as day, and then in popped Martin Luther, German theologian, 1483–1546. As they walked to the exit, she was saying, There were terrible fires and riots and the whole downtown area was trashed for a long time after his death. The motel's the National Civil Rights Museum now. But things only really started to happen down here after Elvis died. The history's real bad – poverty, and a lot of disease –

the place was a pest-hole after the Civil War, and the racism, and now all the trouble with uninsured sick people with nowhere to go. It's only when you go north that you see how bad things are down here. And the truth is, nobody gives a damn.

Off the plane and on firm ground, he was relieved to the point of feeling light-headed, and he asked Hannah where she was staying.

At the Peabody. I took a suite there and couldn't change it – conventions up the wazoo right now. My business partner, Miriam, was going to come with me, before going on to Charlotte. He stood back so she could go ahead of him and then relaxed as he became part of the effortless walking toward the baggage claim. There was a sense of being underground what with all the planes out there, squadrons ready to take off at a moment's notice. The atmosphere lifted, becoming flirty and warm, and he took her bag and carried it, moving closer to her body. And he began to feel it again, the way he had on the plane when she'd crossed over and sat next to him when the plane had come down: the comfort of a woman's body, the stability that comes from touch. The proximity of her arm and thigh, her warmth, and the way a few tendrils of her hair reached over and touched his cheek as if seeking attachment – her way of whispering, You okay? – had righted him when he was disorientated, knocking out the apprehension, that waiting-for-something-to-happen that was so unbearable these days. To distract himself from the sexual tension he admired her stride: it was the walk of someone who knew exactly where she was going. She might push you out of the way at times, but she was able to adjust to his signals quickly, as if in some intuitive way she was tracking him. She was walking ahead of him now, and her hips moved from side to side in a way that was as hypnotic as a clock's pendulum. It took him back to a clock on a wall above a mantel and his father winding it and how he'd wait, eyes wide, for the hour to strike and the cuckoo to fly out with the song of the forest in its mouth.

Outside, in the fresh air, Hannah knew the city and, since he didn't, he was happy for her to take charge. In the taxi, which was incredibly warm after the frozen city they'd left behind, he sat close to her and regretted that he'd not been more together – more of a man – in that weird experience on the plane. He was embarrassed for a moment, but he had no control when the panic kicked in. It was hard to get used to that. She'd taken a somewhat protective role and he regretted that, too. He wanted to kiss her on the mouth. He wanted to make love to her. He could feel his body leap and, when she leaned forward and spoke to the cab driver, he smiled at the backs of her legs, and introduced himself to her thighs, approving her neat waist, and her hips, straight but ample. She was a woman who hadn't had a child yet, he seemed to know that. He remembered the baby's silent face on the plane, but it was just an image, nothing more, gone in a flash, though it left him with a melancholy feeling he couldn't place.

Hannah asked the driver to turn the heat down a bit, and then sat down, her hand grazing his. I have a dinner tonight, she said, but, if you like, I could make it early and show you Beale Street. It's sort of tacky, the street, but the music's pretty cool. We could ride the trolley . . . or – she frowned – are you tired?

Not at all, he said.

When they got to the Peabody, he thought there was something unreal about the place. The opulence of the vast lobby and bar, marble floors and columns, stained-glass

24

ceilings hemmed in with dark beams, chandeliers, and vast arrangements of flowers – the whole thing made him think of a rococo castle, like something out of Florence or those pictures you saw of European cities before the war. The piano was tinkling away and, what with the furniture – heavy and somewhat Bavarian – it all seemed out of time and place. Hannah, with a shrug, said it was just Southern, upping her slight drawl. Kurt was looking round, taking careful note of the entrances and exits, checking to see where the elevators were located and how many floors there were. He caught sight of her hair haloed by a single light at the reception area, and walked over. She turned from the desk and moved toward him with a smile. He took her bag and she his arm, but now that they were inside the hotel, the gesture felt chummy rather than intimate. They moved toward the elevators.

I'll take you to your room, he said, what floor?

He pushed the button with 9 on it. He saw her screw up her nose for a moment, hold her breath and then gasp softly, almost sneezing and trying not to, and he was filled with extraordinary tenderness, so much so that he leaned across and kissed her on her mouth.

4

A few hours before dawn an alarm woke him, far away but insistent, and it left an echo in his brain. Most nights he was only able to sleep for two or three hours and anything could wake him – a car taking a turn, someone opening a door or rain on the window. He'd lie in the darkness for hours, listening, his mind empty, waiting for something to happen. Right now, fear was the dominant emotion and it created a sense of breathlessness that made it impossible to sleep. He'd tried the over-the-counter sleeping stuff, which worked for a day or two before the cycle started up again, and now it occurred to him that perhaps he should explore the darkness: he had an image of his hands reaching ahead of him, holding something off but also moving towards it. He caught a glimpse of a window, and a bed. There was a face on a pillow, eyes wide open, weeping, and he felt his heart would break.

At dawn, waiting for the first bird to sing, he couldn't stand it any longer. He got up, dressed quickly in the dark and began stuffing things into his bag, then tipped everything onto the floor. It was then that the keys fell out. He stared at them and turned them over, one large brass key and a smaller one on a ring. He tried to locate them. Nothing came to him, but he thought they must be the keys to his apartment in New York. He wondered if he'd vacated the premises or just walked out the door and locked it behind him. He was about to chuck the keys into the trash, but he saw three doors in a row, all white, all closed, followed by a feeling of confusion and grief followed by no feeling at all. He put the keys back, slipping them into a side pocket of his bag. He began to re-pack his things, putting the dirty things at the bottom and the new clothes he'd bought the night before on top.

Hannah had taken him to Beale Street, which was low-slung and rough, separate from the rest of the city, almost ghettoized, with the towering Fed-Ex building dwarfing the stores, restaurants and bars selling barbecue and soul. The intensity of the music in the blues club flooded his mind again and he saw Hannah's face looking up at the band. It was impossible to speak, wherever they went the music was too loud, but it was easy, somehow, just to be there and let his mind drift. It allowed him to visit a past that had nothing to do with his own: sounds of the Mississippi Delta and the evening train, juke joints and back porches, low dark dives and gospel singing in the Get-Right-Church, empty cotton fields, lives abandoned and entangled in a lonely and mournful past: *I'm a great long way from home . . . goin' down South. Goin' your way. Did you ever love a woman and you don't even know her name ?*

He walked from his part of the suite into Hannah's room and sat for a moment on the edge of her bed, looking at the shape of her body under the sheet. Last night, when the two of them had come back to the hotel, it was late and she was somehow separate in a way she hadn't been on the street or strolling in the scruffy little squares where musicians older than Dylan were playing guitar for shuffling middle-aged white folk from out of town. And how could she not be wary of him? He was surprised, and thought she was too, that she'd offered the other side of the suite at all, though she'd made her terms clear. Here, in the quarter-light, he could look at her arm in its white nakedness, and her hands with their small red nails and her shoulder that led to an edge of lace. He walked over to the desk to write her a note. *Hannah: Can I see you when you get to Birmingham on Thursday? Sorry to bale this way. I'll explain later. Thank you for being so kind. I'll call you. Kurt.* The night before she'd given him her business card and had written two other numbers on the back in a spontaneous gesture while they were drinking coffee at midnight. They'd been holding hands and he was relaxed, the way he knew he used to be. He'd made her laugh a few times. She'd surprised him in all sorts of ways: her mind had a far reach and it moved quickly, like fingers playing scales rapidly, with no false notes. But then there were those odd dips into a kind of wistfulness that seemed a little out of character in a woman so well put together. He was grateful that for some hours at least he'd been free of his own peculiarities. Going to the gym earlier had helped; he'd exercised for an hour and swum twenty laps and something about the sweat and the heat had got rid of the crash landing. He saw scribbled on the hotel notepaper a scattering of words: *The two major speech areas of the brain are Broca's area and Wernicke's area.* There was a scratch diagram of the brain and another scribble: *Can lying ever be called real communication? Isn't it more like non-communication, a perverse or debased form of speech?* He read it twice and wondered when Hannah had written it. It was so precise and she'd been rather smashed the night before, but he admired the depth of her interest in the work she'd chosen.

She rolled over and threw her arm out like a gesture of surrender, and her hair, heavy and matted in the darkness, covered her face in a way that disturbed him. On the side table he saw a tortoiseshell comb with a silver edge. He almost took it. He didn't know why he wanted it. The glass

28

of water he'd filled for her was still full, the black document lay on the floor, unread, her boots were standing up, waiting for her feet to fill them. He touched her hand, and pulled the sheet up to cover her exposed neck. As he did so she turned again so that she was lying on her back. He wanted to put his hand on her belly. For a moment he saw it round and pregnant, radiant as the moon. His desire to make a child with her was so intense that it tore into him. He quickly picked up his bag and closed the door behind him. On the other side, the empty hallway extended both ways and he couldn't remember whether to turn right or left to reach the elevators. The urgency to get going, to get out, was back: he began running, hearing his heart thud as loudly as his feet, and when he reached the elevators he hit the down arrow furiously, Fuck, he hissed, fuck.

By the time he got to the lobby he'd managed to pull himself together. He strolled over to the night concierge and asked him to arrange a rental car. It was barely six in the morning, but the man was resourceful, had a buddy at Alamo, there were always cars, wouldn't take long, grab a seat and a coffee, not a problem. As they waited, the concierge gave him a map and directions to Graceland, he also insisted Kurt visit Little Rock as well: You gotta admire Clinton, what a guy, I mean, even now, he looks like the king even though we already have one down here. He had his problems, but he sure knew what he was doing, had a brain, the country wasn't about to tank back then. Kurt smiled and nodded, but offered nothing. When the car came, it was a VW, not the cleanest, but okay. Kurt asked for directions out of the city, but the concierge was talking too fast and it was hard to grab hold of the words. Make sure you see the river before you leave, the concierge called after him. The car was waiting

29

and he got in, opened the windows and headed out, relieved to be alone, a little nervous about his destination, whatever that might be.

He didn't want to take 55, but couldn't find his way to 49 either. He was trying to get to Riverside Drive and the Mississippi River, but seemed to be driving in circles. Eventually, he gave up on the river and tried to get out of the city, traffic was building and so was his agitation. Going south to Helena, he found himself on back roads where people were hanging about on corners piled high with garbage and cardboard boxes or loitering in cafés, gas stations and fast-food joints. He was startled to see people walking along the highway. He couldn't remember ever seeing that before, except on a television screen when refugees came walking out of New Orleans after the hurricane turned the city into a lake of floating bodies. He pulled over to ask directions from an old guy with rheumy eyes who was walking against the traffic, pushing a bike piled high with possessions. There was some heat to the day and the old man was struggling. Kurt leaned out the window and asked him how he was doing. The pale brown face fell into deep wrinkles; sweat pooled in lines that fanned out like a delta. He smiled and said, When I woke, sir, I knew I was blessed.

Kurt drove on, leaving Memphis behind him. He was looking at what passed him by: hand-painted signs, often mawkishly decorated: Memphis Wrecking, Lucy's Pawn Shop, Hair from Heaven, Dr Seth Loves You, God Heals and Jesus Saves, Taco Bell, Dixie, KFC, Discount Cigarettes, Ice Cold Beer, Fresh Cut Meat. He could just as easily be in Africa or the Caribbean, and stopping in at a grocery store for a coke, he looked around him at shelves of canned food, cigarette cartons in huge glass cabinets, sacks of rice and sugar, jumbo packs of frozen chicken pieces and bits of pig in jars, the total absence of a green vegetable or a head of lettuce, the cheapness of a cup of decent coffee, brains and biscuit on a breakfast menu. Out on the open road, riding down the Delta Blues Highway, there was nothing but empty fields with the wind sighing through the leaves of dusty, sorry-looking cotton bushes. Kurt blasted up the radio and out came: *Forty years of sufferin', forty years of pain.*

Soon he was surrounded by huge billboards advertising casinos set back in the empty fields, down a dusty road or next to the highway. The billboard-women had magnolias in their wavy hair and diamonds round their throats; they held fans made up of dollar bills and wore clothes that were throwbacks to the 1940s. Coming up were the grand new casinos – white-and-gold castles on a flat plain surrounded by deadbeat little towns shuffled up to a diner or gas station, fields adorned by a collapsed barn smothered in ivy that hid a sprawl of dead cars and rusty water tanks. Shredded cotton scuttled across the road as balls of cloud bobbed just above the horizon. The radio moaned: *The hardest thing I ever had to do. Was holding her and loving you.* The occasional town passed him by, vanishing in a minute, flat, brick houses with corrugated-tin roofs, an armchair on a front porch, an old woman walking along a track to nowhere, arm in arm with the ghost of a Confederate soldier. The radio kept him awake: *Tomorrow I'll hate myself. But tonight I'll be lovin' you.* Nothing but the lonely highway, straight, empty, slipping in and out of mirage; he drifted and veered across the road and then shook himself out of his stupor and slipped Wagner into the slot. The car vibrated with the aching melodies of *Tristan and Isolde*; he played it full blast, hoping it would dispel the ghosts. But if there were ghosts they were only a blue curtain blowing in an upstairs window, two broken steps where a child had once tied her shoes, a hot plate lying in the dirt on which fried chicken had once browned in lard, a bed where a dark hand drew the blinds of two blue eyes. The ghosts receded and he drove relentlessly into the glare, unable to get Hannah out of his mind. She'd somehow taken over his body, too, as if, in spite of her containment, there was a powerful physical and emotional connection that now in her absence felt broken. It was painful. He remembered the quick way she'd speak at one moment and how, at the next, her voice would soften and slow, ending up almost breathless. He wanted to make love to her with the same rhythms. He was filled with longing for the way she pushed her fingers through his or took his arm, the way she leaned across the table as if to whisper something and then kissed him on the mouth. The shape of her breasts under the silk nightgown. Her mouth, thinking quietly all to itself, willing him to reach into her and break the silence. He was tormented by the memory of that night when she'd lurched over in her sleep and her tangled hair had covered her face, a triangle of light across one cheekbone. He saw her body sprawled in abandon: his mouth on her throat, her breasts in his hands, her body on top of his, under his, her face cradled by his shoulder. He was hot. It was hard to breathe. His desire was ferocious and all he could think of was her arched and naked body, her head thrown back in ecstasy. He pulled off the road and told himself to get a grip: Stop, eat something, take a break. He realized the loneliness of the driving had replaced the endless walking in New York City.

He pulled into a roadside diner. It was crowded and as

he entered the diners looked up from their plates; on the juke box Ray Charles sang, *Here we go again. She'll break my heart again. I'll play the part again. One more time.* Walking to a table at the back he felt foreign. A young woman came up, notebook in hand. He couldn't understand a word she said, but asked for a sandwich and a coffee. He looked around at his eating companions who, though it was barely twelve, were devouring mounds of brown meat submerged in gravy, piles of rice, potatoes and a swamp of collard greens merging with some kind of yellow mush that took up every inch on their plates. He felt inadequate in appetite, got up from his table and strolled over to look at the walls, which were covered with old photos. One was an aerial view of some town or other, an old, blurred black-and-white shot with splotches for trees, dark streaks for a railway line and a road, and squares and rectangles that seemed more like facades than actual buildings. The roofs, windows and upper floors were missing as if the shot was taken after a conflagration. The waitress came up to him carrying a plastic glass of water and said, Tha there pichta was tha fire. He smiled at her, moving on to a map which in large black letters announced itself as

H. V. Kaltenborn's New 1940 War Map of Europe, 4th Revised Edition, Rand McNally, Chicago.

He studied it for a while. **Be Sure, Pure** was written in bold at the bottom. His eyes weren't focusing too well, but he followed the black curved arrows: France occupied by Germany, Poland annexed by Germany, Belgium occupied by Germany, the Netherlands occupied by Germany, Denmark and Norway occupied by Germany, and, in an inset, a list of Germany's African occupations: South West

33

Africa, German East Africa, Cameroon . . . on and on . . . He went back to his table, feeling nauseous. The waitress smacked down a sandwich soaked in gravy and bulging with cooked beef, next to it a stack of French fries in danger of drowning.

He drove on for several hours, stupefied by the glare coming off the shiny green plastic covers on oblong blocks of cotton. Nothing but grass and scrawny cotton bushes, wooden telegraph poles and narrow drainage canals, small clumps of cotton caught in the hem of the asphalt road, ragged children staring from the steps of a broken-down porch. A green warehouse with three broken green doors which, when he looked again, had become white ones. The Cotton Processing Company was quietly falling into ruin. There was a cemetery on a rise with a couple of cypresses trapped inside crumbling white walls, and a tiny white church: *Men and women of Jesus Christ, we are truly saved from Sin. And we do possess Holy Ghost Power. Do not be Amazed. Do not be Afraid.*

Around Cleveland the soil blackened and some trees appeared. Kurt slowed down. He'd been searching for the Mississippi River ever since Memphis, but since he'd cut down the centre of the state he'd been nowhere near it. He looked at the map and changed direction, heading east and determined now to find the river. Hours later, after his eyes were tired of looking, it was suddenly there, running swiftly between tall trees. The river became full and heavy, with rushes and cypresses up to their waists in water. But it couldn't be the Mississippi. How could it be, out here next to nothing but delta dirt and wavering fields? In a flash the water was gone. He'd passed it, or it had vanished, leaving him wondering if he'd dreamt it the way these days he so often dreamed of a wide river with barges and pleasure boats dotting the surface. But the river in his dreams had a city on either side of its banks, with spires, turrets and towers piercing the blue sky. He veered off the road and slammed on the brakes. He'd just had a clear image of a wall and on it was a print of a German city near a river, and it was the same river as the one in his dreams. It struck him that the river he was looking for out here was the Elbe not the Mississippi. He felt disorientated and sat quietly for a while, his head back, eyes closed. Out of nowhere he saw a red sky and a woman walking with her hair on fire.

He took out his map and spread it across the wheel, trying to locate himself.

The numbers on the map were reassuring, 82 to 61, then down south to Rolling Fork; at Vicksburg he'd have a good shot at finding the river, certainly at Natchez. His eye strayed, left Mississippi and crossed the county line into Louisiana where he saw, out in the middle of nowhere – Tallulah. He was ecstatic. He forgot the river. He could get to Tallulah from Vicksburg; there was a two-lane highway, or he could take the Interstate and, if Tallulah had a phone booth, he could call Hannah from her home town. Now he knew where he was going.

5

He drove from Tallulah to Birmingham to see Hannah, and on the way sent her a vase of white lilies. It was two days since they'd been together. He was absurdly excited and anxious. When he checked in, he asked for the number of her room and walked past it on the way to his own; behind her door he could hear piano music and small thuds, like rocks falling on soft soil. The Chopin took him to a concert in a garden with a view of mountains in the distance, but he didn't know where or when. He stood outside her door a moment, listening, then walked to his own room where he sat on the bed and tried to think how best to approach her. He couldn't concentrate. His body was full of agitation and there was a pain in his chest. The thuds he'd heard coming from behind her door kept repeating in his mind and for a split second he saw a woman's face tilted upward, holding a baby above her head and laughing. He shut off the air conditioner and opened the windows. The Alabama air was soft and warm, the first breeze of early spring stirred the lids of the buds, the sun shone hard and bright. He closed the door behind him and walked quickly down the hallway to Hannah's door and knocked.

When she opened the door, she was out of breath and her hair was a nest of coils on top of her head, her cheeks were rosy, her forehead beaded and damp. Kurt thought she looked a little like Georgia O'Keeffe in one of those photos Stieglitz took immediately after he'd made love to her: that vulnerability in the eyes and a sense of being unfairly exposed. Hannah's hands were on her hips and she looked at him with an expression he couldn't decipher, half smiling, half not. The music had stopped. I came to apologize, he said, leaning forward to kiss the far end of her cheek. May I come in? She moved one hip to let him through. Thank you for the lilies, she said, turning her body sideways in the direction of the vase. She stood with her back to the door as he looked round the room. Her clothes had been tipped onto the bed and the nightgown she'd worn in Memphis lay in a sprawl, the buttons of the bodice loose, its fullness white and voluptuous. He saw her inside it, arms flung wide as she tossed in the night, dreaming things he couldn't fathom. He wanted to be inside her the way she inhabited that nightgown. He could imagine a future where he walked by the water with her, and they slept together under a tin roof with monkeys clattering above their heads, and woke on a morning like any other, beautiful in its ordinariness. She came up to him and he took her in his arms and they held each other until he could feel their bodies relax.

She was wearing black yoga pants and a pink tee-shirt. What were you doing just now? He thought she'd been running, though her feet were bare. Dancing, she said, raking her hands through her hair so her face was an empty beach. He smiled. Of course, he said. Should have known. It was obvious by the way she moved, or rather how her body moved for her, giving every gesture a precise economy and grace. I'd like to see you dance sometime, he said, bringing the future into the moment, making her smile. He was aware that she was looking at his body: his hair was wet from the shower and he was conscious of the newness of his blue jeans and the dust on his shoes. The rooms are identical, he said, looking away from her gaze and up at the

37

walls. There was tension in his body and a vibration he was sure she'd pick up. He wanted to grab and hold her hard.

Are you staying here? She asked it carelessly.

Four doors down.

He caught a flicker of hurt in her face. She folded her arms under her breasts.

He looked directly at her. She hadn't recovered from the way he'd left her and now that he was with her, the flight out of Memphis made no sense to him.

Where've you been? She was back to neutral and, as she walked over to sit on the bed and yanked the black band from her hair, he saw it tumble about her shoulders and felt an ache, a separation. Her face was lost to him as her body curved forward and she rubbed her ankle.

I just drove all over the place, he said. No particular direction, just checking the place out. There's not much out there but traces of foreign occupations and the Lost Cause. He came over and sat next to her. She was still a little breathless and her body was hot and energized. And, he said, taking her hand, I went to Tallulah.

Oh, she said, closing in on herself, as if he'd caught her naked.

Found no trace of you, he said, staring at her face which, in that split second, became the face of another woman sitting at a kitchen table, late at night, who said, I can't do this any more. Hannah's face returned and he surfaced with it. We lived outside Tallulah, she said, on a scuffed piece of dirt with a muddy creek at the bottom of the fields. Barely visited the town, except to go to the grocery store or post office; the hospital there'd likely kill you. She paused and, when he said nothing, she went on with quick strides as if trying to get to the end of this. Didn't go anywhere else for that matter, though – she looked up at him – I ran off to

38

Baton Rouge one night with a boy to see the Mississippi. A thin strand of gold was snared at the edge of her mouth and he longed to move it, to touch her skin, to kiss her. She blew the strand away.

Did your father actually farm there? It looks bone dry. He could hear his voice, but the image of the other woman lingered and her words echoed ghostily in his mind.

He didn't know how to farm, Hannah said. He was just on the run. One day we were in this house in Atlanta, the next minute he was bankrupt and it was all gone – not a bed or a chair left – just the debris of our lives chucked all over the lawn. White trash overnight. Refugees. He was listening intently now. My mother, she said, the day we left, was sweeping the front step like a demented hausfrau and my grandmother was yelling at my dad that he'd made us into displaced persons, and meanwhile he was chucking everything into a pick-up truck and screaming at my brothers that he wanted to get the hell out of Atlanta and never put foot in it again. She stopped, looking ahead of her for a minute. She tucked her legs under her and her body became tight and spare. When we got to Tallulah, there was a beat-up old farmhouse and some cows and chickens and a broken-down shed full of dead machinery. We looked around us and no one said a word. There wasn't even rage, just a dumb kind of shock and inertia for months on end, my mother silent all the time, and my father so angry you'd catch fire if you stood too close.

I'm sorry, he said. I can't imagine that kind of dislocation.

Yes, you can, she said quietly. You're in it.

He was startled. But you pulled out of it. How d'you do that?

Made damn sure it wouldn't ever happen to me.

39

And money helps?

Money always helps.

Does it take the pain away?

Some.

He crouched down in front of her, took both her hands and looked at her until she brought her face up. Hannah, he said, I need to tell you something. I lied to you.

She stared at him, and for the briefest second she caught the edge of her lip between her teeth and bit down on it.

I lied to you, he said. Did you know?

She moved quickly and shoved him out of her way. He was so affronted that he wanted to grab her by her shoulders and pull her back. Don't say anything, she said, walking away. He stood up. If you knew I lied, he said, why didn't you ask me about it?

Doesn't work, she said tightly. Only makes things worse. She was at the bed, rooting through her things like an animal digging a hole in the dirt.

He smiled ruefully. Have I become one of them to you – one of those corporate liars?

This is different, she said, with her back to him, And you know it. Her cheeks were hot and her hair flickered red and gold.

A lie's a lie, he said flatly, so I'm no different, not really, from the people you deal with every day.

She stopped, turned and gave him a cool stare. *Are* you a corporate thief? Is that it? Is that what you're running from?

She knocked the breath out of him. No, he said angrily, I was in finance, but I wasn't into corruption. I know the difference.

She breathed out. Okay, she said. Okay. At least that's clear. It's just that I don't want to lie to *myself*. And I could.

So I'd prefer if we dropped it for now. After all, we barely know one another.

I've hurt you, he said.

She walked over to the window and looked down at the tops of trees. When I woke up, she said, and you'd gone, I persuaded myself that it didn't matter, that nothing had happened between us. But, in the middle of a meeting . . . She turned to look at him . . . while I was doing a presentation . . . I froze, couldn't speak a word, because I was convinced you'd forgotten me. He went over and put his hands on her, drawing her toward him, so he could see her face. I'm so sorry, he said. I've not had to take in someone else's feelings about what's happening to me. I've been trying to get through the days, the confusion, but I haven't seen the effect of what's happening to me on someone else before. I'm just trying to deal with it. I've screwed up with you. But I wouldn't forget you. I couldn't.

Maybe not, she said, softly, but you left. He could feel the electricity in her hair as her head dropped for a moment.

Look, he said softly, let's have dinner and talk. Can we do that? There's a restaurant downstairs. Okay, she said. As she was moving away, he grabbed her hand and pulled her back. Don't let's mess this up, he said urgently. Her hand was like a live wire, and his heart began to thump wildly the way it had in Memphis. The speeded-up sensation of that night returned, both exhilarating and alarming at the same time. To calm down, he took a few deep breaths. Look. Why don't I clear out and let you get dressed. I'll be back. He grinned sheepishly. I promise I'll be back. In fifteen minutes on the nail. That okay?

He was back in ten, and paced back and forth outside her door, checking his watch every minute. When he knocked, Hannah walked out as if she'd been standing right there; as she turned to close the door, he asked her in a domestic way, Have you got the key? And, before he knew it, a sturdy oak door appeared out of nowhere, complete with brass fittings and the number, 102, in a fan of glass. He remembered the door in a vague way, feeling comforted by it without knowing why.

As he walked with Hannah to the elevator, he began talking about Baton Rouge, where he'd spent the night, walking by the river for hours, going to the library, reading the history of the place, talking to people, scoping it out. And she in turn told him about the boy she'd run off with to see the Mississippi River, which gave him a clear view of her first sexual experience. Perhaps, he said, we should go to Baton Rouge together, and to Natchez? I'd like that, she said, as she walked down the hallway. And, as he stepped aside to hold the fire-door open for her, he noticed how she kept glancing at his ring finger and the indentation that was no longer there.

At dinner, she asked him no questions, just sat eating her flounder and pushing the spinach round her plate while he talked to her about where he'd been. She looked a bit preoccupied but wouldn't be drawn out. He began to worry about how the night would go. That last time, in Memphis, when he'd unexpectedly come through to her room, long after the doors between their rooms had been closed, she was reading. I couldn't sleep, he said. Mind if I sit down? She moved her body and sat up on the pillows. He pulled up a chair. He'd understood she wasn't going to get pulled in by any vulnerability of his, and certainly not by sex. He'd got an impression of love affairs that had ended badly, men who'd been jerks or hadn't shaped up. In the silence now, just as in Memphis, some energy was pounding away and he was trying to work out whether it was his, hers or a combination. He'd first been aware of it in a dive on Beale Street, when they'd been sitting at the back, far from the band, in leather chairs, and it was loud, hot and crowded in there, but there was an intimacy about the space, the way there is in a movie theatre, all those people, and yet a sense of being alone together, as if everything was a backdrop, blurred and without reality. She'd remarked on how often he moved – how he'd just get up suddenly for no reason, and then come back to sit beside her, taking her hand, holding it, moving his fingers between hers and then letting go. She'd said it was kinda flighty. He'd stayed put after that, draping his arm lightly across her shoulder and down her body as if to listen to her heart, and then moved his hand down her arm, brushing her thigh. He'd touch and un-touch her, and these moments were filled with the most exquisite sensations, passionate and tender, urgent and fleeting, creating an intimacy that felt as if it had always been there. Back at the hotel, she'd pulled away from him and he'd followed her cues, even the most subtle, and accepted the bed in the other part of the suite, and yet the distance between their rooms had vibrated with an energy that was almost magnetic. Much later, after a very soft knock he'd come in and said he couldn't sleep. And then in the morning he'd gone.

At dinner, when he couldn't stand the awkward silences another second, he said, Can we talk about last time?

Which last time?

In Memphis, when I asked if I could sleep next to you and then bolted in the middle of the night.

Sure, she said.

I need to explain, he said, shoving his plate aside. I didn't know I was going to bale any more than I knew where

43

I was going. I mean not a clue, like when I left New York the day we met. I don't know if it's claustrophobia or what, but it's only when I get out – the minute I was out of the city, the minute I left Memphis – something lets go. Before, there's a tremendous sense of danger. As if the cities are wired. But when I'm driving those straight empty roads out there, I feel fine. It seems okay not to know what's going on. I see it as having some purpose. But I also flip out of time. It's like I remember what happened down here: I see the floating casinos but remember flatboats carrying slaves, cotton barges, the transportation of the dead . . .

Hannah looked across at him. I can't tell you, she said bitterly, how much I hate the South. He waited. I'm sorry, she mumbled, I just feel on edge here, I always do. He took her left hand and moved his thumb and forefinger across the joints. No rings, he said, feeling the deep throb of desire right back where it had been before. She looked directly at him, Let's go, she said, I don't want coffee. Do you? Don't drink it, he said, standing behind her chair, pulling it back, waiting for her to pick up the large black purse she lugged around with her. The tension was unbearable.

44

∽ 6 ∽

In the elevator they didn't speak. He was going to tell
her how he'd lied, but it felt risky, particularly after hearing her reaction to his leaving her in Memphis. She was
less steady than she seemed: the family disaster, the
financial ruin, the father's madness, and the language
she used to describe it – hausfrau, refugees – it felt load-
ed. He didn't want to put her through anything more. He
thought they intuitively understood one another, but his
life had crashed in a different way from hers and he was
a long way from understanding any of it. At her door he
hesitated, but she said, Come in, we can talk a bit. Sorry
to be so twitchy at dinner. There's something about that
restaurant, the glitzy style of it, the Southern-ness, that
gives me the heaves. I'm not usually so jumpy. Her voice
was soft and he was grateful. She unlocked the door, put
a light on and walked over to the sofa and sat down.
Above her head was a reproduction of Manet's painting
of the stark-naked woman reclining in the woods with
two men wearing black suits, and she with her long,
naked foot placed between his grey trousers, there, and a
basket of peaches tipped over, peaches strewn over a
silky, sumptuous bodice, a blue-dotted dress tossed to
the side. For a moment his head spun. He went over, sat
next to her, and looked her straight in the eyes and said,
There was no head injury.

No.

You knew?

45

I don't know until someone tells me; saying it makes it real, before it's like a ghost floating around that you keep bumping into. She seemed as composed as the naked woman in the woods. She leaned forward and pulled off her boots: I didn't bring any other shoes, she said, tilting her head in his direction, and these are killing me. He caught a glimpse of translucent flesh, and then of black, broken skin, and a bandage darkened with blood, people walking, soldiers, slaves . . . walking . . .

She looked up. So you didn't go to a doctor?

No.

She turned to face him, tucking her legs under her. So what exactly's going on?

I seem to have lost myself, he said quietly.

She said nothing for a while and then picked up his hand and stroked his fingers. When exactly did it start? And where were you?

I remember being on the subway, getting off and walking to an office building. When I got there I didn't recognize it. I knew I was supposed to go in. But I couldn't. His breathing was shallow and his heart was beating fast. I walked right past. That was the beginning. I couldn't remember anything before that. I didn't . . . He stopped . . . I didn't remember who *I* was. His head was down. He hesitated again and looked at her. If there'd been a blow to the head, he said, something logical, something to explain it, but one morning, there was nothing there. Nothing. It's impossible to describe . . . the emptiness of it . . . the absence of any meaning without memory. Like falling through space. One time a man came up to me on the street and called my name. I hadn't the first idea who he was, but he obviously knew me. He was pissed off. It was scary as hell. I thought I might

46

not recognize anyone . . . So I kept my head down, kept on walking. It's only in the last few days that a few images have come back, but I don't understand what they mean. He was quiet again. That same morning, he said, I started walking and I just kept going: I walked over a hundred blocks and ended up in a run-down part of town near Battery Park. I spent most of the night there, zoned-out and adrift, but I remember seeing people whose lives had gone completely off track: drunks and addicts, homeless people, refugees from reality – a whole lot of destitute people living in squalor with no sanitation, running water or electricity, just huddled in ruined and abandoned buildings, shelters made out of garbage and broken doors. I'd no idea why I was there, but I thought maybe my life was going to end up that way. It didn't seem to matter. I was just an observer, my life and everyone in it had gone, and the only thing I could do, the only thing I felt compelled to do, was to keep moving. I walked for most of that night.

And you just kept going?

He nodded.

And you don't know what set it off?

No.

She moved a little closer to him and touched his arm. Could it be post-traumatic stress? Are you a Marine? Could you have been in Afghanistan or Iraq?

None of the above.

How can you be sure?

I'm sure. His voice was clipped.

Did anything happen? Anything sudden or traumatic?

Not that I'm aware of.

Her voice softened, becoming more concerned and he

shifted with it. So you don't actually know why you left your job?

I know I'd begun to hate the whole corporate thing. I can remember general stuff better than personal information. Like that my French is pretty good. That I like the Red Sox. Have a thing about hospitals and doctors, but I don't know if I always did. Cops scare me these days and I don't think they did before. But why I couldn't face going in that day, why I walked past my office and left everything behind me – no idea.

D'you remember what kind of work? Finance, we know, but what precisely?

He was grateful for the 'we'.

Venture capitalism, maybe?

He wasn't interested, could barely respond, and was left with a sense of distaste. It's like . . . I have some kind of grievance . . . with money.

And you only know where you lived from the address on your driver's licence?

Correct.

You've never gone back?

Immediately he began to feel spacey. No, he said. I thought about it, tried to, but couldn't make it, couldn't even go to that part of town without setting off a panic reaction.

And, I guess, she said, cautiously, there may be a wife or a child that you left behind you?

His face was stricken for the merest second. Then it went blank.

She put her hand on his arm. He slumped forward, his hands on his knees. It's okay, she said softly. We don't have to do this . . . maybe it's the wrong thing. His body locked. The tension was like a band, steely and cold, and he had to

48

remind himself to breathe. After a while, he said, It's why I lied to you, there's no other way of explaining the amnesia or filling in the gaps, of explaining *myself*. If I don't give you answers it's only because I don't know them. The day-to-day stuff has gone – what I did, where I went, what I thought and felt, it's pretty much all gone. New info stays, but my life before has disappeared. He looked at her. I thought you'd be more pissed off about this.

I didn't understand, she said, you seemed like a guy on the run, in flight from something, you seemed sketchy, as if you were hiding something. She smiled. And I'm a sucker for complicated guys. And, she said, there was something gentle and nice about you. The head thing didn't altogether make sense, but after a while, I sensed there was something wrong rather than that you were being a jerk.

He got up and went to the bathroom. Washed his face with cold water and came back. All I can tell you, he said, is that most of the time I function, I'm fine, no one would know, but now and then images come up and the problem is they're so damn *real*. They seem to exist on another dimension, real-unreal. Once I saw my mother walking with me, I knew it was her, and through that image my name came back to me. Hannah looked confused. Well, I've been using this name, of course, he said. But it didn't seem like my name. I wasn't attached to it. I couldn't say whether I belonged to the name or even if I belonged to myself. It was the name on my ID, so I used it. But for a while I gave myself a number.

What was it?

102. But, however many times I wrote it down, it meant nothing to me. But then, standing outside your door earlier on, it morphed into another door and the numbers, 102,

49

were set in glass above it. That's the address on my driver's licence: 102 West 75th Street. When I can fit two pieces together it helps me feel less crazy. And, he said, his face looking pained, the last thing I want is to seem crazy – to you, or to me.

I understand, Hannah said, but I don't want you to think that I know more than I do. Memory's very complicated stuff. And – she laughed – I'm really only a lie-buster.

He hesitated. Can you, he said, stay with me for a while?

Like now?

Yes.

I can do that.

He covered his mouth with his hand and above it his eyes were deep and still. He touched her cheek, It seems too much to ask, he said.

That I'll stay?

He nodded.

Because you'll leave? That's what you mean, right? You want me to stay with you until you go again? And – she shrugged – well, we all have our abandonment issues, don't we? She hesitated, and then she sat up on the sofa with her knees crossed, facing him. She seemed very young suddenly, her knees like that, the bones sharp, the skin pearly. Okay, she said, tell me what happens, as much as you can. He moved closer and put his hands on her arms. There's something I need to know from you. You never did tell me if you were divorced?

I got divorced five years ago, in 2001. August 17th, to be precise.

What happened?

Nothing ugly, she said, Just a relationship that neither of us were brave or honest enough to fight for. One of those painful relationships that became more so.

How long were you married?

Four years. He was bipolar, more lows than highs. An attention-junkie, had to take up all the oxygen in the room, had to charm everyone who came his way. I didn't have the patience for it. She looked away. There was a lot of love once, mutual interests, happy times, but nothing that seemed to hold.

A failure of courage?

I think so. It could've worked, and that's the frustrating thing, not being able to make that happen.

You dating anyone now?

No, she said, I have to watch my rescue fantasies.

He laughed.

I suppose, she said, leaning sideways against the sofa, for you, all that is gone? Can you remember anyone back there you might have been with?

He tipped his head back and closed his eyes for a moment. No. Sometimes I get a jolt, not of memory, but of feeling, and – he hesitated – a sense of betrayal. And I wonder about that.

It's almost a metaphor, she said, amnesia, for the man on the run from commitment, connection – the stuff that drives women nuts. He smiled. You think I'll keep baling on you? He looked steadily at her. It's not about that. I've been wandering longer than I've known you, and right now I can't guarantee I won't do it again. Putting it that way makes it seem like I have some bizarre affliction or condition or . . .

Well, you do.

Do what?

Have a condition . . .

He put his hand on her knee and she jumped slightly.

He removed it. Maybe it's not as complicated, or as simple, as a condition, he said. But whatever it is, I don't want to know what it is. Not right now. She was quiet for a while. Well, the serious problem is that we don't know what kind of relationships you may have back there. She ran her fingers lightly up and down his arm and pushed through the gates of his fingers until their hands locked. Your memory will come back. And then what?

All I can tell you is if there was a marriage, it feels over. I could be wrong . . . but I think I'd know something like that. I'm more concerned that I can't promise not to leave, because I don't seem to have any control over that. But, maybe I could tell you where I've got to? His voice was apologetic. Keep checking in?

She smiled. You'd like me to not take it personally? Her hand touched his cheek, moved round to the back of his head, where the hair was soft and light. He needed a haircut. She slid off the sofa, crouched down and began to take off his shoes and, for a moment, he wondered if she was trying to steal them, but the thought was so bizarre and so transitory that it may never have been a thought, or not his thought anyway because he'd no idea where it came from. The minute her hands were on his feet, he relaxed. He pulled her up against him and kissed her tenderly and more passionately, moving his hands through her hair. He got up, grabbed her hand and led her over to the bed. His hands landed hard on her hips and he pulled her against him, and with the certainty of his touch, her body seemed to fold. She ran her hands over him tentatively, exploring his shoulders and arms, moving up to his face. He grabbed her from behind and kissed her, tipping her onto the bed with its sealed scarlet covers and barricade of starched pillows. He got on top of her, reaching over to pull a pillow down. Lift your head, he said, and watched her hair scatter into red and gold. He stared, mesmerized, as her fingers undid the small buttons on the scalloped edge of her blouse. His attention was riveted in a way it seemed to him it hadn't been for months or years or ever. He rolled the soft cotton away and snapped the front clasp of her bra and watched her breasts tip out like peaches. They were exactly as he'd imagined them when he'd sat beside her or across from her or conjured up her body during those long, empty hours of night-driving or walking down long white roads straddled by cotton fields. Her nipples were hard and they tasted sweet. He wanted to bite them and make her scream. Her hands were gentle at the back of his head, moving to hold his face, as if to restrain him, but when he kissed her, her hands slid down to yank up her skirt. His hands polished the long expanse of her legs, and moved up the insides of her thighs and across the smooth slope of her belly. Her legs opened and his tongue flickered over and inside her as her body arched and then shuddered. Her voice was small as if caught in a jar. She drew him back up and he stopped and looked into her face. He was watching her as she kissed his cheeks, eyes and mouth, small sipping kisses lingering at the edges of his smile. She lifted her knees to welcome and enclose him, and all the time she held him with her eyes, not looking away or turning her head as he entered her. Her arms cradled his back and he brought his mouth back to hers as she shuddered and climaxed, again and again. He heard himself cry out with a sound he didn't recognize. The intimacy shocked him, leaving him breathless and

53

amazed and, as she closed her eyes for the first time, he touched her cheek, which was hot and pink, and smoothed back her hair. His head rested on her shoulder and her arms held him still.

Danke, he said.

They went walking for an hour or so, stopping for a drink in a bar a mile or so from the hotel, and then walked back. He liked it that she could keep up, that her legs were strong, that he could hold her hand and kiss her every time they made a stop or turned a corner. They were sitting on a bench backed by a small park when she said, Why'd you speak to me in German just now? You've never done that before.

Don't know. He was light-hearted and felt close to her. Why d'you want me to be Jewish?

She shoved her hand through his arm. I don't know, she said. It's not that I married Jewish or even live Jewish or anything like that, but I'd still like it if you were.

But why?

I guess it's that you're German-American and I'm German-Jewish-American.

And?

I didn't think it was important until I was attracted to a German who wasn't Jewish. She laughed. How interesting is that. She got up and he followed her. My little brother, Hannah said, used to call German the cruel language. Her voice dropped. When they say those words in the movies, when the actors with the blond hair say Achtung, Blitzkrieg, Gestapo – when I hear those words it's like all the uniforms and boots and swastikas come tumbling out of a dark closet and I want to run. Because I'm one of the Juden. You say you're not and that makes me scared of you being German – German extraction or whatever, but we can't even say that with you because you're straight-through German. You feel it. It's not something you've forgotten. And to add American to German doesn't do it, because even if it's slipped in among all the other mongrel names that have been changed and replaced and made-over, we Germans know that we can't hide from German. And, for Jews, even those of us who've been turned into born-again Christians – what we want above all to hide from is German without Jew. She stopped. He looked at her and wanted her to keep going. There was something about her voice that was speeded up, running ahead of itself and away from the past. My grandmother, she said, survived the war but couldn't talk about it, something about a particular kind of German shame shut her up, and instead she was this pathologically enraged human being, shouting words from way back she thought we didn't understand. And my mother, even though she knows nothing about what happened to her family in the camps, has a deeper horror of all things German than her own mother. For years I thought she was really fucked-up about it – worse than my grandmother – who spoke beautiful German, had read German literature, and was able to preserve some love of it through the literature, the music. My mother preserved the hatred as if she knew what had happened without hearing the words.

But there are other words, Kurt said, reaching over and kissing her on the side of her mouth. *Du bist meine kleine kartoffel.* She looked up at him: You speak German?

I know the words, he said, half surprised, half not.

I know the words, too. Her eyes filled with tears and she shoved them off her cheeks.

56

Did your grandmother, he said, taking her hand, trying to get her to walk more slowly, speak German to you?

Sure, but when she spoke it my mom would only answer in English. It was a hidden language between the two of us. Hannah stopped dead in her tracks. He turned to face her. What? He waited and when she spoke again her voice was low and dark. I just remembered . . . *how* she taught me German . . . She'd take me into the closet in her room and we'd crouch there, hidden, and she'd whisper the words and I'd repeat them until I got it right . . . That's how I learned German. I don't know why I've never thought of that before. He held her against him for a moment and stroked her hair. She moved back and turned slightly to one side before walking on again. When I was about seven or eight my mother heard us and it was like she'd caught us in a dirty secret. She took my grandmother out of my room and screamed at her, I don't want to hear it. Can't you get it? It's not my life, it's yours. Get over it. Years later I secretly started reading German classics by myself. In high school, when my dad's business really started to tank and home was the worst place to be, I went to the library and started taking out those monumental books and reading them, and then I bought paperbacks and hid them under my bed, like porn. My grandmother bought me a Collins German dictionary that went under the bed too. My mom found them one day and chucked the whole lot in the trash. And if ever a peep of Wagner or Mozart came on she'd flip the channel or leave the room. Hannah's voice slowed. But I heard another language, too, which was my grandmother's code language for atrocities . . . and she used those on my mother. She could be cruel, but in English – the cold language. She looked at him. We know, for sure, that you're not a Jew?

57

We do. He shoved her gently: Give it up.

What?

My not being Jewish.

How can you be sure?

I guess I know it the way I know I'm a man. I don't think that particular religion runs in my veins.

Maybe religion's in the blood, the DNA, something like that?

It's carried in memory and feeling, and with feeling you don't have to know things, they're just there.

They'd reached a bridge, and he stopped with her to look over at the water. I read a case history once, she said, when I was studying psychoanalysis, about memory and silence. What haunted me was this story of a family from Frankfurt after the war. The grandfather and father had been Nazis, but when the war ended the father covered all traces, so that at the time of denazification, when they were getting rid of medical personnel with Nazi backgrounds, he managed to remain a doctor, and he and his wife, their small daughter and the grandmother, none of them ever breathed a word about this, destroyed all traces, promised each other they'd never think about it. Until one day, years, years later, in Texas, the mother, who'd been the small daughter, walks into her bedroom and sees her two young sons goose-stepping up and down with swastikas painted on their tee-shirts, and when they see her, their arms jerk up and their hands push out flat and they scream: Heil Hitler!

Never been told?

Not a word.

Pretty scary. Sort of unconscious transmission?

Skipped one generation and surfaced in the next.

She walked on but he was feeling disorientated. Let's go

back to the hotel, he said, walking ahead of her. He felt a jolt of pain, and got snared in an image of a woman standing by a bridge. The woman had dark hair and looked about twenty; she was laughing and she called to him and then climbed onto the iron railing, balancing there a split second before diving into the swirling water. He was pierced with guilt, nameless and deep. Hannah had caught up to him, she pushed her hand through his arm and into his pocket, moving her hand against his thigh. He closed his eyes and the woman's face with its sleeked-back hair emerged out of the water. Her silvery arm waved at him. He blinked and his head cleared. They walked back to the hotel in silence and went up to Hannah's room. She took off her boots and he walked over to her CD player and put in some blues music they'd bought in Memphis. Come dance with me, he said. He held her tight. *When I'm standing on shaky ground. Will you love me just as I am?* There was something about the way he held her, steadily, that guided them through the uncertainties of the night. He was a good dancer and so was she; sometimes he led and sometimes she did. He put on some Bob Marley and made some moves to impress her; she picked them up immediately and added some of her own. He was laughing as he spun her and pulled her body back to him so fast that she gasped. He suddenly saw himself at a high school prom moving smoochily to a Motown tune with a girl called Molly who'd ruined an entire summer for him. And he was smiling about that when Hannah stopped abruptly and asked him when he was leaving.

Not tonight.

Tomorrow?

He hesitated. Probably.

Why?

I need to go to Tennessee he said.

Why Tennessee?

Not sure, just feel a pull in that direction. I won't be gone long. And you're going back to New York anyway.

She put her hand on his arm. I'm fine with anything as long as I know, so tell me when you're going, will you? Wake me up. Promise?

You got it.

≈ 8 ≈

February 17, 2006

Dearest Hannah,

It's two o'clock in the morning. Planes are flying in the dark. I'm writing to try and calm down. I've asked you to hang in with me and now it seems weak, but somehow you're mixed up in it. I love you. I've no doubts even though all we really have are the hopes we have of one another which don't add up to much more than moonshine. But the feeling's very strong and was right from the start. I don't know what it is about you, your face, your body, the quick puzzled smile I get from you that makes me want to be near you. It's as compulsive as the walking used to be. You may see me as someone it would be a whole lot better to stay away from, someone who can only complicate a life you've dug out of hard dry dirt. But from the moment I decided not to move my seat on the plane and you decided to smile at me, I knew I had to be with you. And so it begins and who knows the ending? And this pen in my hand and the hotel notepaper, and the plain simple need to record something that has happened before – but to whom? And when? Sometimes I think I've slipped out of my life so I can enter someone else's.

I'm trying not to bolt. I have to explain this as I go along or we'll lose one another. There's something about 2 in the morning that's full of dread – for a sound, a scream, a siren to go off and for everything to start moving horrifically fast. That's when I start walking, not like in the movies

61

when the soldier is told, Go, Go, Go, but in a way where I have to watch everything and be very careful where I put my feet because nothing is solid. At 2. At now. Right this minute. I'm trying hard not to run. I'm trying to get back to the anchor that's you holding me and me knowing you're still breathing because the sheet's rising with your body's rhythm. There were three of us once. I'm talking about someone who was once part of my life and family – someone who's gone. I don't know who.

I'm in the overwhelm again, just like on the plane. It's like a horse rearing up with its hooves crashing against a stable door with fire whooshing up his legs, but I don't see the fire or even the horse, just the feeling of an animal going crazy with fear. One time, when I was about five, a rug in my bedroom caught fire and the flames began to climb up my bed. I was so transfixed by the purple and blue and red I couldn't move. Someone swooped in. I see arms lifting me up and my face looking backwards over a shoulder. The person carrying me is silent. The rug vanished and there was a new one. I remember setting fire to the rug, but no one asked how it started.

Hannah, you said I should go back to the city, give my address to a cab driver and tell him to take me there. You said I should google myself. I can't do either. I don't want to know. In your face I catch a look of doubt, of alarm, and then it's gone and you manage to reassure yourself that I'm okay. Am I dangerous? Have I done something to someone and can't remember? Do you wonder this about me and not say? In your terms, that would mean you're already lying to me. Please don't. I can take your questions even if I can't answer them.

You told me you've made mistakes, and you don't want to make another one. I suspect you've chosen the same kind of man or turned different men into the same kind of man. You said you've had enough of Type A men and CEOs who loot and lie emotionally or married men with their lethal ambivalences. You get pulled in by the loneliness. You rush in to save. But what are *you* hiding? You ferret things out of me and I let you because when I begin to talk things come out of nowhere. I need that. For the first time in weeks, things are moving a bit. I believe you when you say it's most likely temporary. You don't hide things from me and you seem willing to tell me anything, even the things that might create too much of an impression, like that you haven't spoken to your parents for years. And that your brothers are all over the place, and there's only one of the four you see at all. Fuck-ups you call them, losers. I winced when you used those words even though I don't see myself that way. I know what's happening to me has meaning, I just don't know what it is.

You make me laugh when you talk about your family. You put on your grandmother's voice with its German traces and tell me how she screams down the phone at you for not speaking to your mother when it's enough already that she should be living with a lunatic surrounded by empty fields and people who've never heard a cello or read Thomas Mann or listened to a symphony or heard a foreign word without saying, Huh? And then you flip it all aside so quickly, you stop and slither over so that before I know it you're asking about *my* mother. Else Altmann. My mother. I say it a few times and look at it from all angles. Does it fit her? Do we fit together in this name? Are we a family? Is there a father, a sister or brother? Are they dead or alive? The image of my mother and me walking comes up and I have that brief vision of her and its tangible, like the way you began to kiss and kiss me, covering my face, blotting my cheeks and eyes and forehead all over, leaving me dizzy and damp. I keep trying to find my mother. If I go back to the road we were walking on and follow it, I get one frame, like a chord of music that's stuck. Where is she? Is she dead? The thought's terrible, like being surrounded by dense smoke and everything's burning. And now I'm wondering if my mother's name has a soul that belongs only to her. Is she alive? You asked me that in the soft but neutral way you have and I liked that because if your voice had in it all your feelings about your own mother it would be impossible to bear.

You haven't touched the word, love. But I know you love me because your body told me so, and I couldn't have touched you if I hadn't known that. Your body remains with me, beautiful in its shapeliness. It's what I've thought of all the time since I saw you outlined under the sheet that first night. When I left and went driving around for hours and hours not stopping I thought about you all the time without knowing who you were. I was thinking about you and your body with longing, wanting to hold it and know it, wanting you. It was so painful I had to pull off the road. Now I know you it's worse. The longing's unbearable. My fingers know your nipples and the small knot in you, the silkiness that leads all the way to your womb, the sound of your voice caught in a gasp, the orgasms that shake you, each one pulling me more deeply inside you. No one has looked at me that way. Nor I anyone. That kind of intimacy is rare and it's real. I have to hold to what's real to stop slipping.

Two in the morning, no planes now, but street lights that reach into sleeping homes where children roll into one another and a baby bawls in its crib and a mother drags herself out of bed and shuffles through the cold, hugging herself to the baby . . . and now I've got snagged on the word, baby . . . cold fear . . . the mother is walking past all the things she sees but never notices: things that have been collected, like a cup with a rose painted on the inside, a pen that's never in the same place, and the scissors that no one but her ever puts back in the jar near the sink. She looks at the lamp with the chipped funnel, the clock that stopped dead when the picture fell, the books side by side, hundreds of them, waiting to be read; the stove waiting to heat the soup and warm the bread and the lights waiting to come on after the darkness. And if all this was gone in an instant? The way it was for you when they came to haul away all the things that had made up your whole life? You said, They're only things. But without them, when the house is empty or gone, burned alive or washed away, when nothing's left to say you ever lived there – how do we go on? How do we know who we are?

Sometimes, right this minute, at 2.20, I feel on the edge of knowing something. I keep pacing up and down, waiting. I can't go out into that hallway, or walk down the stairs one by one or read the fire warning inside the elevator. I'll freeze or run. And sometimes I have to hang onto the sides of the doors not to be sucked into the vortex. The only thing that persuades me to stay till morning is the solid beauty of your body folded into the sheets, your head weighing down the pillow. My only certainty is if I wake you, you'll put your chin in your palm and whisper, What's up? Come to bed. Tell me.

9

Three in the morning. Gone. Like fingers prised off a cliff edge, Kurt let go. And he drove like a maniac through the empty night streets, somehow ending up in the rubble and wreckage of a ghetto where ghosts were hanging out in alleyways and people were sleeping against charred broken walls or lying under shelters made of plywood and milk-crates. A few men stood huddled at a highway underpass as if waiting for buses to take them away. When they saw his car a few wandered towards him through the darkness of the unlit streets, shuffling through smoke, silent, bowed. He almost hit an old guy in a blanket and skidded to a halt. He went to check on him and recoiled from the filth and fragility, the stench of urine and death, the fingers bent like twigs. He wanted to shove the whole lot of them back under the underpass and drive away. A woman was slumped over in a wheelchair and didn't seem to be breathing. A child cried out for water. Predators lurked in shadows; behind the scaffolding of toppled refrigerators and dead cars, a family huddled around a fire, boiling something that smelled appalling. He'd hit a place-warp, slipped into a nightmare. It left him slack-jawed and shaken, unsure where he was, what country, what century, where?

Once out of Birmingham he could breathe again, think straight, even consider going back to the city to see Hannah again. He stopped to call her and apologized. She didn't say much. You've moved back quite a bit, he said.

She said she needed to think. This was difficult. Maybe too difficult. It made him panic. He tried to explain to Hannah how a point came and he lost control, what that felt like. She was listening carefully, and he could feel her thinking as he was trying to explain. But what exactly *happened*? She asked it more than once. I panic, he said. It's like I can't think. I just react. What set it off? I don't know. It may have been a plane in the sky or a sound or smell. I know it does-n't make sense. And you're right, I did promise to wake you and tell you. I'm sorry, the most I could do was write to you . . . The sense of urgency, of danger . . . I can't explain . . . It's like I'm running for my life. Are you will-ing, she asked, to think about . . . trying to get to the bottom of this? When you're ready, she added quickly. Otherwise nothing will get better. I know, he said. And then, sudden-ly, the tension was gone. It was as if she let something go and by the end of the conversation they were close again. He felt righted. He promised to call her. He'd get control of this. No question. The sun was shining. He was on the open road. And he was in love. The city was behind him. The ghosts had vanished into the sweet southern light and the radio soared with the sustained, mighty voices of the Mississippi Singers: *There's a man in my soul, He will bear my burden and heavy load, just keep talking about Jesus.*

He drove south on 65. He wondered if he'd ever been in love before. Was he using it as an escape from the question of who he was? Maybe that's all it ever was. Things seemed slow and easy now. It was a huge relief. He won-dered if it *was* physical, after all, not a blow to the head, but something neurological. He wondered if anyone was looking for him. The woman with dark hair who dived into the river and waved? The police? Was his picture on 'America's Most Wanted'? He laughed out loud. He drove quickly and then slowed down when he reached Tuscaloosa, where he took secondary roads and stopped in small cafés to eat and call Hannah from pay-phones. He drove hour after hour taking in occasional beauties that time had left behind: a country store with gas pumps that hadn't worked for decades, and prices that made the mind boggle. Baptist churches, simple and white, nestled up to cotton fields, a cypress-planked gin shack was entangled in telephone wires and vines, a woman in blue hair rollers was standing in the doorway of a front porch, screen door in ribbons, red dress and pearls bright against the ebony of her skin and the dull wood of the porch. He was listening to Ray Charles, the early music, before the orchestra came in and the raw went out. At times he felt light-headed, but he put it down to happiness. He called Hannah and hated the disembodied voice of her message and not being able to see her face, but was determined to stay connected.

He travelled as far south as Monroeville and then went way over to Enterprise, on up to Anniston, and to the edge of Georgia without crossing the line. When he was too tired to drive he pulled into a motel and slept, sometimes at midnight and sometimes at two in the afternoon. Sometimes he drove all night and had breakfast in a truck stop. Wherever he went, he avoided talking to people. Once, out of the blue, a woman asked him if he was looking for someone. The question threw him because it seemed true. When he came to a place where he could settle for a while, he avoided anyone who might engage him in talk or ask him questions. But then it occurred to him that since no one knew him, he didn't have to cover his tracks any more. He could be anyone from anywhere. He could create a new identity, begin a new life. Far better

than going back. The wildness of his thoughts both comforted and confused him. When he got going again it was
without purpose or direction; there was a vague sense he
was being led somewhere, but he didn't know where. If he
saw a cop, he gave him a wide berth. He kept rigorously
within the speed limits. Once, an ambulance siren made
him veer off the road and he almost landed in the ditch.
When he needed money he didn't use a bank ATM – something more off the beaten track, like a dollar store or a
small pharmacy or convenience store. He avoided the bigger towns.

After Madison, he cut across to Florence and crossed into
Tennessee, staying well away from Memphis or Nashville.
The slippage began not far over the Tennessee line. He was
tired, slowed by the rhythm of southern voices and the
endless driving. His eyes were dull from watching the
road. He tried to discipline his thoughts but couldn't. They
began to collide, fragments of music caught in a broken
web of talk and laughter, words whispering and repeating,
images rushing in and sidling out. He drove on, thinking
occasionally of pulling into a motel to sleep, but not doing
it. In the end, he forced himself to stop at a sleazy bar on
the edge of a small town to rouse himself. He walked outside in the cold air and then went into the bar. Inside it was
murky and dark, the bar counter wet with beer and littered with froth-stained glasses and congested ashtrays.
He sat at the far end of the bar and ordered a coke. A
woman came and stood beside him and he tossed her a
brief smile and looked back down again.

Don't I know you? she said. He looked at her. He was
taking the question literally, then caught himself and
laughed. She became more direct. He declined. She

shrugged and walked off. Too bad, she said, turning her head back to look at him. You're cute and I could make you happy. People were staring now and he finished his coke and got up to leave. As he was moving to the door she smiled at him again and without knowing why he asked her name. Liz, she said, turning her back to the counter, resting her elbows on it, so that her breasts were like an offering. Elizabeth? he asked. Sure, she said, if you like it better. He felt sadness and regret as an image began to form through a blurred lens. He didn't try to blank it out: he was trying to get a face, a voice, anything that might explain the grief that kept welling up from nowhere . . . and he was in a room with orchids in brass pots, talking avidly to the woman who'd dived into the river from the bridge. Same woman. Same long dark hair. She was telling him about a deal she'd just pulled off, some financial coup. She was leaning toward him and they were celebrating, laughing, holding hands. She was so happy and seeing her that way gave him comfort. Then she stood up and he saw she was pregnant. She couldn't. Couldn't be. He recognized the dress, black with small pleats falling from below the breasts. He remembered buying it. How much it cost. He went cold and his mind snapped shut.

It was cool outside the bar and he walked across a field to a broken-down barn where animals had once been sheltered. There were empty cans and pizza boxes in one corner. A filthy mattress in another. A pile of straw and manure had been shovelled out the door and he nearly stepped in it. Under a tree lay the shrivelled carcass of a lamb. He couldn't look at it. He walked back to his car and drove on. The headache started up when none of the towns he was passing lined up with his map. The landscape began to break up the way in his dreams images

70

would shatter till his mind was like a broken windshield. He'd left the highway without knowing it and found himself wandering deep into nowhere. The soil was spent and it looked like no plough or tractor had broken it, no brick or floor, no remnant of house or store, no church on a distant rise, nothing to place it in time or memory. He stayed there, his hands flat to the earth, trying to pick up a rhythm. No bird sang. No wind blew. Had it been a place of slaughter or battle? Did its desolation come from what lay beneath its surface? He sat with his knees up, his arms and head down. He got back in the car and after a while was on the highway again. Up ahead was miles and miles of nothing. In his head the same.

The landscape was greener, more boggy, there were ponds and creeks, pastures with cows grazing, an occasional grand house set back from the road with red barns behind it. An hour or two later it was pastoral and lush, with tended fields, green meadows and small lakes half-hidden by oak and cedar trees. Baptist churches and flat houses gave way to truck stops, motels and malls, industrial parks, gas stations and fast-food joints. He saw by the names that he was driving over the killing fields: beneath the grey asphalt lay the remains of the Confederate and Union dead. They lay, arm in arm, united in death, their bodies falling in slow motion into trench graves that closed over them in the mausoleum of time. The front lines had been taken over by auto-muffler shops and urban sprawl, a pizzeria had wiped out the memory of a day's carnage. He took a turn off the highway onto a small dirt road which wound down into a copse of cypresses and winter trees that had begun to move into spring. Here, in a small Confederate cemetery, with stones pale and beautiful in the dwindling light, he read the names of the dead: German, Italian and French names, boys between sixteen and twenty, at peace together among the small, square headstones, the roar of the highway a stone's throw away.

Back on the road, he pressed his eyes closed to clear his vision. He was dizzy and his head was pounding. He was weaving, his hands shaking on the wheel. A sign up ahead announced the name of a town but the glare from the approaching cars blinded him. Lights began to flash behind him. When they came closer, he put his foot down hard on the gas. The siren started up but he didn't stop until the police car was right alongside and the officer's angry face was yelling at him to pull over.

10

There was a wide red circle with a smaller blue one inside it. A nurse was taking his vital signs. He could make out the oblong of a window, blinds, a dark night, rain pounding the window. A pilot's face in a leather helmet behind dark goggles. The cop had gone. Kurt lay in a hospital bed, and he felt calmer; his head was clearing. He was able to sign the papers, answer the nurse's questions. This your name? Kurt Altman? Yes. And you live at this address? This your insurance card? Yes. And you told the police officer you didn't know who you were? Lost your memory? That what you told the police officer? Can you have your wallet back? Well, no, we like to keep valuables locked up in the hospital. It's just policy. You must have it? Well, you'll need to sign off on that. We can't take responsibility . . . Now, sorry to bother you with this, but can you tell me if you've had a blow to the head recently? Car crash? Anything set this off? You've been through these questions before? Well, can you tell me how long since you knew who you were? Maybe four weeks? Okay. The police officer called your home, but there was no reply, no message machine. No family? Uh-huh. Wife, children? Parents? Sibs? If you've lost your memory, Mr Altman, how d'ya know that?

A doctor took over: Police officer said you were speaking in some other language, Mr Altman. He thought maybe German. Is that where you're from? You think so? Okay. Well, I'd like to do some tests. I'm Dr Lehman, by the way. Yes, I am Jewish. Got any feelings about that? No. Okay. Well, there are just a few more things we need to check out to see where we are with all this. Some tests might help.

What tests?

Well, the diagnostic work-up has been done, after you came in from the emergency room. You remember that? Good. Okay, so we've done the blood work, X-rays, thyroid function tests, spinal tap, CAT-scan etc. Well, they may seem odd tests to you in the circumstances, but they're the right ones. Yes, I'm sure. The results? There were no abnormalities, Mr Altman. And the neurologist looked you over, too. Dr Schmidt, I think? Good. Thing is, we need to have you taken to the Baptist Memorial in Memphis to get the rest seen to. No? Why not? Well, sure, you can have the rest done in New York when you get back. Sure, I understand. But just because you get the all-clear on the organic components doesn't eliminate a lot of other things . . .

Like?

Psychological tests, that kind of thing.

What kind of thing?

Well, there's the Dissociative Experiences Scale – the DES – and a Structured Clinical Interview would help clarify things . . . and we could . . . Yes, I'm a psychiatrist, Mr Altman, you seem to be exhibiting some anxiety right now. Perhaps I've been asking too many questions. I'm just trying to eliminate a few things. Don't see how that could be a problem. You're right, we can work together on this. Sure. Okay. So no Memphis right now. You'd like to stay here. I'll see what can be worked out. Mr Altman, how're we doing here? Okay? Good. Look, I know you're tired, but, can I just ask you again if you've been treated for this condition before?

No.

Gone to an emergency room?

No.

Seen a physician about it?

No.

Okay. That's it for now. Seems like a good thing you got picked up so we can sort this out. I'll come by in the morning. I presume you want to know what's going on? Not sure you do? Okay, that's fine. Let's wait on things a bit. Just rest up for now. I sure will. See you in the morning. We could give you something to help you sleep? No? Sure. Right. No problem.

In the early hours of the morning Kurt found his clothes, put them on, and, leaving everything but his wallet behind, walked out of his hospital room. He stood outside the door, listening, waiting. All clear. Not a sound. Only the muted lights. He walked carefully down the silent hallway past the other rooms and made a right into the lobby. It was empty. Scarlet and blue tropical fish slid between plastic vegetation in a tank full of bubbling water. He walked swiftly through the automatic doors, past some beds of pansies and saw to his right the MRI Diagnostic Center and to his left the Emergency Center where he'd come in earlier. It was quite cold; there were deep puddles and sodden grass, but the rain had stopped. He walked nonchalantly past the Sleep Study Clinics, leaving the hospital with its red domes behind as he walked quickly to the traffic lights at the end of the hospital complex. On the right was the First Assembly of God and on his left the Little General Gas Station. He made a left, entering the highway on the shoulder. The road was straight and empty. There'd been a storm and the road was strewn with broken branches and leaves. He walked for about eight miles and then was forced to make a decision: up ahead was a cluster of road signs and the one with 22 on it decided the matter. He crossed the highway under a bridge and followed the sign for some miles, perhaps three or four, head down, occasionally looking up and taking in the odd detail on either side of the highway: a derelict barn, a house or two, mostly green fields and fences. The road began to feel familiar the minute he caught sight of a real-size model of a white horse on the other side of the road. There was also a sign announcing the name of the town. He couldn't make out the name in the dark but thought this was the way he'd come when the cop had pulled him over. Soon enough, he saw a Budget Inn with a mess of mall across the way. He was walking briskly now, keeping his head down. His shoes and feet were soaked through and his feet were burning. He walked into the motel parking lot, stood outside the office and rang the bell. An Indian man came out and let him in. Kurt said his car had broken down a mile or two up the road, and after showing his licence and American Express business card, found his own way to 124, where he took his shoes off and fell asleep on top of the covers – flat-out, dreamless.

Four hours later, at about 8 a.m., he reached for the telephone and called Hannah in New York.

Hannah?

Where the hell are you?

Okay. Listen. Yeah, I know. I can explain. Hannah? Look, let me just tell you what happened. Okay? Try not to be mad.

Just tell me you're okay?

I'm fine. Got picked up by the cops. Not an accident. Just kinda lost it. Had some kind of a breakdown.

What kind?

I don't know. Headache. Sweating. Feeling faint. I don't know. Just came over me. It was after I left Alabama, was just fine down there, but things started falling apart when I got to Tennessee. That's where I am now.

What happened?

I was disorientated, lost my bearings, just driving for hours on end like a zombie, landing up in Civil War cemeteries, spaced out, feeling peculiar, having this sense of the dead being right there, like I was driving over them. All I could do to keep on going like I was supposed to get somewhere. Then this cop started flashing his lights and made me pull over. He thought I was over the limit.

Were you?

Of course not. But I hit him.

You *hit* him?

Yeah, I did.

D'you often hit people?

No, of course not. I was in a panic and he was being an asshole. He was asking me questions and I couldn't take it. Anyway, I passed out. He took me to the hospital.

Were you hurt?

No, I asked him to take me there because I didn't want to be dragged to some police station in the middle of nowhere, that's why. Being a northerner is pretty much like being a foreigner down here.

You're sounding a bit paranoid.

Well, perhaps I am – of cops who pick you up in the middle of nowhere.

It doesn't sound like you – any of this.

I know. Look, I'm sorry, Hannah, I know you're worried. Everything kind of went out of my head after Alabama. I called as soon as I could.

Where are you now?

I'm in a motel on the highway.

D'you want me to come?

It's okay. But thank you. I appreciate your asking.
Hannah, I'm sorry about this mess, but I'm going to get
out of it. I've not morphed into one of your brothers.
Please don't worry. I know it's a bit bizarre, but I'm basi-
cally okay. I miss you. I think about you all the time, really
I do, but sometimes you get tangled up with all the other
barbed wire in there and then I forget to call.

Barbed wire?

Just meant the entanglement of it all. I have to get
checked out at the hospital. Get my stuff out of there. And
then I'll get going.

What happened at the hospital?

Well, I told the doctor I had amnesia, and didn't know
who I was. He didn't seem surprised or anything. They
did a whole lot of tests, asked me a ton of questions and
then, later, I walked out.

You checked yourself out?

Well, not exactly.

You just walked? Why?

Hospitals spook me. He saw himself in a hospital emergency room wringing his hands. On his lap was a small
blue hat.

When was this?

About two in the morning. Usual time. Look, I'll keep
in touch from now on, I promise. I don't really know
why I panicked in there. They wanted to take me to
Memphis to do more tests, and that bothered me. And I
thought the police would be trying to find out who I was
since they'd got my ID. Anyway, when I got out of there
I started walking down the highway. It was very peace-

ful. Very few cars, it's out in the boonies here, just high-ways with flat houses, junk food and gas stations, end-less trucks, Church of Christ chapels all over the damn place. It's desolate as all hell. The cop who pulled me over said I was talking German. Can't remember if I was. I was a bit out of it by then . . . You okay, Hannah? You sound upset.

I *am* upset. I don't like to think of you going through this, especially by yourself. I don't understand why you started walking again. People don't walk down highways. After a pause, she asked anxiously, Are you still there?

Yes, I'm still here. I'm just listening, that's why I'm say-ing nothing.

I have to tell you, Kurt, I'm finding this hard to under-stand. I mean, we were together. We made love. It was beautiful. I've never felt closer to anyone in my life. You said you'd tell me if you were leaving, but you didn't. You wrote me a letter, but it was sort of broken off. And, once again, when I woke you'd disappeared.

I know. I'm really sorry. I called you many times and then I didn't call you for almost thirty-six hours. I under-stand. I left messages. I know you hate messages. I do too. I knew you had meetings. I realize you can't call back because I've lost my cellphone, but I did try to stay in touch until I hit Tennessee.

What's with Tennessee?

It's where I kinda lost it.

But you said you were going to Tennessee.

That's right, I did.

It's such a massive flight response, she said.

I didn't think of it that way.

I wonder if you're in some way trying to make me feel what it feels like to be you?

79

Not sure what you mean?

Well, you're confused, lost and all over the place and now I'm feeling like that, too.

I'm not trying to hurt you, Hannah, you have to believe that. Last thing I'd want. I love you. D'you know that?

Yes, but I'm still confused.

Hannah?

Yes.

Look, I'm sorry, I have to go. A cop car just pulled up outside. It's the same guy. I'll call you back soon as I can. Please don't give up on me. I couldn't make it without you.

Can you at least tell me where you are?

I'm at the Budget Inn.

Where?

Don't know. Hang on. Let me look . . .

Kurt? You still there?

Yes.

Where exactly are you?

I'm in Dresden, Tennessee.

11

Kurt walked to the door. The same officer stood there with
the same expression. You trying to give us the runaround,
Mr Altman?

No, officer. I fully intended to go back to town. My
things are still at the hospital, in Martin.

How d'ya get here?

I walked.

No one walks.

It's simple: just follow the highway and you end up
right here.

I'm taking you back in.

Sure thing. I'll get my jacket.

We're going to the hospital first and then back to the
police station. Sure you can hang around that long?

After he'd done the paperwork at the hospital and had
his feet bandaged, Kurt signed himself out, took a taxi
back to the police station to pick up his car. Once he'd
signed more papers and been thoroughly warned about
hitting a police officer, who was, this one time, not going to
hand him a summons, he went back to the Budget Inn. He
called Hannah, got her message machine and immediately
fell asleep. He slept for four hours. When he woke he had-
n't the first idea where he was. The confusion quickly
cleared but he had a compulsion to walk back into the
town of Dresden, which was less than a mile from the
highway. His shoes were ruined but he had some new
socks in his bag so he took the bandages off his feet and

examined the burst blisters and the raw, red skin, then put the bandages back on, followed by dry socks. He stuffed his feet back into the broken shoes and thought he could manage it. He took a few steps. Walking was painful. His feet were on fire. He got used to it. He walked on the shoulder of the highway to the lights, making a right. In the centre of the square was a new courthouse, with a large marble statue commemorating the Dresden dead in the two world wars, and, at the bottom of the plaque, the names of the Korean and Vietnam dead. Across the way, he noticed the stone Confederate soldier with a lowered gun in his hand. There was a brand new post office close to stores that were thirty years out of date. His feet were now causing him such pain that he went into the hardware store, found some farm boots and took off his shoes and chucked them in the trash. The bandages were bloody, but not much to do about that, so he put the boots on top of the bandages. From the post office he looked down a long street with older houses on either side of it, trees about to bloom and the occasional parked car hunkered down in the late afternoon. All very quiet. He stood there and stared a while.

That's when the slippage began. His head was throbbing. His eyes stared ahead but his vision was blurring. He couldn't make out the name of the street or see any of the houses; they were white blobs, with windows that seemed to lunge and doors that gaped. The trees were black and burned. No one about. No sound. His senses were hyper-alert, but his body had fallen asleep; it carried him like a fish lying on its side in a slow-moving river. He followed the street, head down, eyes half-closed, arms loose at his sides. A car came up and he crossed over to the right and walked in the gutter. After a while the tarmac ran out and he was walking on dirt which was muddy and littered with branches from the storm. There was an army boot lying on its side. And a bundle of clothes that someone had dropped in the mud. He heard a plane and looked up at the sky, but saw only the white flare of its emission. He felt dizzy and stopped for a moment, then looked down at the dirt and then up again to see people walking through a landscape with a red sky overhead . . . a woman in a man's coat carrying a baby, a child slumped over an old woman . . . He put his hands over his ears to stop the screaming, drawing his head down into his chest . . . a vibration began in his brain . . . a train passed in the distance . . . He was freezing but his face and hands felt scalded. The street led him on and he followed it till it ran out. Trees fenced out the light, beyond it was the roar of the highway and beyond that the burnt-out crater of a city with only one steeple reaching into the sky.

On the right he saw a white house with a porch and four steps leading up to it. He squinted up at the windows, eyes recoiling from the glare, the pain in his head quick and stabbing. He got to the front door and slumped down, his back against the white frame, his eyes closed. Carefully, he took off his boots and put them to one side. The bandages were soaked through with blood but he felt no pain. When he looked around him he saw sparks in the sky and heard a deep roar and flames like a tidal wave rolling down the street. He felt only a profound lethargy, a need to sleep. He stayed on the doorstep all night.

In the morning he woke to see an elderly woman looking down at him. She was staring at the bandages, the dried blood and broken feet and she shuddered for a moment, her hand to her mouth. Leaning over, she shook him gently by the arm. Are you all right? He stared at her in confusion and tried to get up. She restrained him. Sit a while. He tried again to stand. No, no, sit, she said, touching his shoulder. Sit a moment. Do you want I should call an ambulance? He shook his head. She crouched down next to him and peered at him anxiously. He kept thinking, this is the worst it's ever been. The woman's voice helped him, it was soft, sort of foreign sounding, Germanic, she was reassuring him that he was all right. He felt better, and began slowly to recover himself. He didn't trust himself to stand, but he looked up at her and tried to smile. Then he pushed his hands down hard on the step and raised himself up. She took his arm, waited for him to steady himself, and led him through the open door. The minute he was inside he felt a surge of cold terror, and considered running back out again. Please come inside, she said. I will take care of your feet. She picked up his boots and carried them in.

He looked around him at a hallway with a door at the end of it. The house had a jamais-vu feeling about it but there was something about it that he knew, just knew. The woman who'd led him in was small and spry-looking, with grey hair pulled back and tied loosely at the nape of her neck. She looked at his face carefully and closed her eyes for a second. What is your name? When he told her, she gave a quick gasp and he couldn't tell whether it was pleasure or pain. He found himself staring intently at her without knowing why. Altman? she repeated. Yes, he said, thinking he'd seen her before. He realized she looked like the woman in the dream he'd had of his mother and himself in a garden, drinking lemonade, waiting for a woman called Trudi. He asked her, Are you Trudi? No, she said, my name is Frieda. But, she said, I have a daughter, my oldest, she is Trudi. He was flooded with something deeper than relief and when she smiled he closed his eyes for a moment. An overwhelming sense of sorrow filled him, so much so that he felt he could float away on it. He was a small boy, and he could feel himself being passed over to Frieda like a parcel. He stared at her and she stared back.

She tilted her head. You don't remember me, do you?

No, ma'am, can't say I do.

She smiled. Well, come, come, she said, standing aside so he could walk ahead of her. It was overcast outside and the house was painted in dark colours, but it wasn't gloomy. He could feel himself coming back; his eyes moved quickly along the wall, glancing at photos of children and young families, graduation pictures, soccer games, that kind of thing. Go up ahead, she said. He found that he was shuffling like a refugee, his steps small and tentative, the pain excruciating now. At the end of the hallway was a large kitchen lit by a garden. He liked the big black stove, the windows with geraniums in boxes, the dark wooden table and the chairs with velvet cushions. There was a fireplace and blue-and-white china plates propped against the mantelpiece. He studied everything in the room, turning to glance at a bookshelf full of German cookery books, trying to remember something, anything – and then out of nowhere he had a sudden flash of a magnolia tree in bloom. He looked through the French doors that led into the garden hoping to find it, but there was no magnolia tree there. He turned to ask her, Have I been here before?

You came here many times, she said, pulling out a chair, but you were a small boy.

How small?

85

From a baby till you were grown. She smiled, I was your mother's best friend – we came together from Germany. A long time ago. She ushered him toward the table. Come, sit. Take the chair with the red cushion. It's the most comfortable. She walked over to the stove where a dark, iced cake sat on a white plate. She brought it over and cut a piece for him. I was going to give this to the church sale, she said, but you need it more. She brought a pot of coffee and two cups and got an enamel bowl and filled it with water and salt. She knelt at his feet and began to unwind the bandages, which were crisp and black. He said quickly, I'll do it. She shook her head. No. I will. She gave up on the unwrapping and told him to put his feet in the water. It will hurt too much. Let them soak for a bit. The water turned pink and then dark red. She looked down into the bowl and up at him, staring. You were three months old, Frieda said, when Else first brought you to me, but . . . she stopped herself . . . I heard you had lost your memory. Is that true?

Yes.

Do you remember coming here with your mother?

No. I don't remember a lot of things.

She looked puzzled. He said, I have amnesia, I'm not sure how or why, but I came to Dresden in the middle of the night and somehow ended up at your door.

Ja, she said, this I know, about the amnesia. You walked from the hospital in Martin down the highway in the rainstorm. In Dresden, she said, you are famous. Everyone is talking about the young man who has lost his memory. It's a very small town, she said. She reached into the water. Please, lift your foot. I can take the bandages off now. So, she tilted her head up at him, You remembered enough to come back to me?

He smiled. I guess. She looked at him expectantly, but he

86

didn't try to explain, and couldn't anyway. She put her hand on his and with the touch of her skin he could see her more clearly. She stood up to get a towel from the drawer and on the way back she reached over and touched his hair. You don't have your mother's curls, she said, and your hair is dark. He took a moment to steady his voice: I don't remember my mother, he said. Shocked, she said, This is true? How can that be?

I guess I came here because I remembered in some way coming here with her. And so, she said, you are here to remember your mother. You want me to tell you about her?

If you're willing. He watched in a mesmerized way as one at a time she lifted his feet out of the water by the ankle and placed each carefully on the towel. She got up to throw out the blood and water. Thank you, he said, you're very kind. The water she brought back was the colour of rust. She smiled – Only iodine. The skin is broken and raw; it could become infected. He noticed now that she was pale as she looked at his feet, waiting some minutes before she asked him to take them out of the water again. You should wear nothing on them, she said. Let the air heal them. They look, she whispered, her voice aghast, like feet that have burned. Then she lifted her head quickly and smiled. You ask me to tell you about your mother and suddenly out of nowhere I see things. The colour returned to her cheeks. She got up abruptly and walked to the sink and stood there a moment. As she lifted his boots off the stainless-steel draining board and put them under the tap, she suddenly buckled over and began to sob. Water was spilling over the edges of the boots and the leather was dark. Kurt was about to go to her, but without turning she put her arm out behind her to stop him. It's okay, she said. Please don't worry. Neither of them spoke. Water ran hard

87

into the boots and she scrubbed out all traces of blood, filling and refilling the boots with water and then tipping it out. She opened the French doors and put the boots in the sunshine to dry and returned to the sink and cleaned it before turning to him.

What can I tell you about Else? The name came out in a whisper and faded away.

Tell me anything, he said. He quickly added, But I can come back. I'm sorry to barge in on you this way. He was terrified she'd agree to a delay.

She walked and sat across from him and, with her hands flat on her cheeks, she wiped her face dry. He looked quietly at her. My mother did that, he said. When she cried she wiped her face with her hands, the way you just did. His voice wasn't too steady. Ja, Frieda said. A lot of what she did is what I do. Frieda poured them both some coffee. I'm glad you've come, she said. I've been waiting all these years for one of you to come back to me. There was a slight tremor in her chin, but then she lifted it and looked directly at him. So, she said. I will begin at the beginning. Is that what you would like? He smiled – If it's okay. Ja, she said, it's okay.

The first time, she said, you came here you were a small baby and every year after that you came. She paused, waiting for a question from him that didn't come. So, she said, putting her palms down on the table. Perhaps I'll try to tell how it was, as much as I can, but it's hard. Okay? She laughed softly and took a deep breath. I'll try another way: I've been in this country since '48. I'm an American now. I don't pretend not to have come from Germany, but I don't say it. I picked up the habit after the war when to say it created a look, as if a flashlight was shone in my face. There are Germans around here, she said, but we are only a few now, and we are old, we are almost sixty years here. This town was started by a man called Mears Warner. He came as a surveyor in the early 1800s to lay out the town. He named it in honour of his father's birthplace, which was Dresden in Germany. So we came here. Not much of Germany left now but the name, not much of anything left here but two highways. The Civil War destroyed this town. It was buried by history, or that's what they say. Now we have only the highways and the malls and the ugliness of new things.

I came here, she said, three years after the war in Europe ended. You must know very little of this, she said. We used to say all the time: after the war, before the war, after the war . . . But now there have been so many wars, other terrible kinds of wars, and you know nothing of my war, only of the terrorist war . . . and the American wars abroad, the occupations.

He smiled to encourage her. I've read a lot about the Second World War, and seen the movies, but there are missing pieces. The German pieces are missing. We don't know those. And I don't know how a German would remember the war, how it was, even though I am one. I don't know what happened in the years after the war ended. It's as if I never went looking for that.

She nodded. We didn't go looking. We needed to forget. After the war, she said, things were terrible in Germany. The first winter after the war ended the ground froze. They had to use explosives to dig graves. People were starving, sick, dying. Hundreds of our generals and officers had hung or poisoned themselves, and many people took that as an example: women who'd been raped too many times hanged themselves in their kitchens and their children cut them down. Young men who had seen the end of the war

89

couldn't face the future. There was no future. And most of us were refugees, walking with nowhere to go. The railway lines were blown up and the bridges were gone and so we kept walking one way and then the other, like demented people. Everywhere we went we were hated, soldiers could do anything to us, and they did. We were like the cities, another kind of rubble. There were no houses, no streets. Refugees who came home found strangers living in their houses and they had to move on. To find work was almost impossible, there were no factories, no offices, no shops or places to buy food. No food even. I got a job on a farm, collecting potatoes. I was the one responsible for finding food, and I used to go through the fields when they'd been cleared and try to find us a bit of potato or half a beet or onion or some forgotten carrot, bits and pieces. We lived on these. Frieda smiled – The word we had for it was *stoppeln*, which means to forage. She smiled at Kurt. You've heard that word before? I can see that in your face.

Sometimes, he said, when you're talking I hear another voice underneath, with inflections like yours.

This will be Else's voice you're hearing, she said. We both came from Dresden, we were all our lives there, we spoke the same. So, she said, let me tell you about her, about your mother. Is this what you wish? He noticed how careful she was to make sure he really wanted to know. Else, she said, was the one who said we had to get out of Germany. We had been refugees together, her mother and mine, who were friends, and she and I, who had been inseparable all our lives. We shared the experience of walking, looking for some place to find safety, to stop. We ended up in the American zone. It was from there she kept writing to the authorities to ask them to let us go to

America, and then she went on the train and waited in freezing, half-bombed offices for days, waiting for permission. To find a way to get new papers was very hard because there was nothing left, no birth certificates, no addresses, no identification, nothing to say who we were, and no places left to show where we'd come from. We'd been burned up with our documents, we had no existence. She breathed in. We had to start again, and everything was slow, slow, slow, and so difficult because no one wanted to help us, or listen to us. They wanted us to disappear or die. But after a year or so the papers did come. Those years between, she whispered, they can't be described, the things we saw, the suffering and starvation everywhere, the way women were treated like garbage, like the leftovers of war. We were spared a lot, being in the American zone, but sometimes we left and went wandering, and we could see how it was outside our zone. Then we came back.

We left there in the winter of '48 and we – my mother and I – came to the South because my mother knew a family who'd lived here from before the war. The thing that I remember is that I felt nothing about leaving Germany, nothing. It was as if everything there was dead and I also, dead, from any feeling about leaving the only place I knew as home. Your mother, Frieda said, she went to New York with her mother. But I didn't want to live in a city again, and nor did Mother. We wanted to live in the countryside because farming was part of our history: my grandfather, he had a farm, and my mother was a child on it – raised on it. I like this word you have here – raised – like a turnip or a cow. So we came and here also I married a man called John Bernard, who was American. He died in '98. He'd been in the army in Germany, fighting us, so he knew what had happened there. But he and I, we didn't talk about that time. He'd seen some of what I'd seen and he knew what had happened to women and girls there. And we were girls then, your mother and I, only fourteen years old when we left. It helped me that my husband knew, that he'd seen. She looked up. Perhaps without this I would not have married. We lived here and had our children in this town. My children taught me to speak American. They corrected my words, but they didn't want to learn my language and once my son, he asked me, Mom, were you a Nazi?

Kurt looked at her. And were you? He could feel his heart racing. Was my mother?

She smiled. That is like your mother, the way you asked. She looked directly at him. Ja, she said, we were Nazis. We were part of everything that happened. My father, he was a member of the party. Ja, he was a Nazi. I was saved from responsibility because I was a child in the war. We have a phrase that absolves us from full responsibility, we call it *der Gnade der spaten Geburt*, which means the grace of late birth.

I don't mean to bring up painful things for you, he began.

I understand.

I just need to know whatever you can tell me.

You get this from your mother, this wish to know. But she and I, once we were here, in safety, we didn't talk about any of this. I wonder if you can understand how that is? It is so un-American. Here it is talk, talk, talk.

Silence is one way of surviving.

For us, it was the only way.

Have you ever gone back?

How could I? One of my children, she went once to Dresden, but I wouldn't go with her. When your mother

92

came to see me here, with you, the past was there in the shadows, it was what bound us together but we left it alone. She smiled, stirred the coffee in her cup, waited a moment. Your mother, she said, her eyes large and luminous, I loved her like no other person, not even my own mother, my own children, my husband, and I loved her this way because there were things we knew about one another that no other person could ever know. She would have walked through fire for me, for any of us . . . She stopped to compose herself. There was a time, Frieda said, when Else put words to what happened to us in Germany – only once – soon after it happened and . . . She shuddered . . . I made her do this, and it was wrong, but I had to do it, or I thought I must because she was suffering so terribly and I thought it would help her. But after she was different – she lost her fire, her anger, the things that had made her strong before. She was just a young girl walking up and down with her mouth stopped and her eyes terrible, as if all the time she was seeing it again. Writing it broke her. I saw that, but I didn't understand what I was doing . . . What you said just now about the different ways of surviving, it was my way, but I should not have done that to her.

It must seem like I've come here to disturb you again, he said sadly.

Perhaps, she said, it's time for that.

Kurt was listening so intently that sometimes he couldn't keep up with her, and sometimes he barely heard her. Her voice faded in and out because it was more than he could absorb. There were questions he wanted to ask and couldn't. Whenever Frieda paused, he wanted to ask if his mother was still alive, but when the words moved from his brain to his mouth he couldn't speak them. But now Frieda was the one who hesitated, holding her hands on the sides of the hot coffee pot, looking down with an abstracted expression on her face. She pulled herself out of her reverie and looked at him. Else used to come, she said, at this time of year, before Easter, before the trees were in blossom, and she would stay with me a week, sometimes more. She hesitated again. I hope you will understand if I move over a bit here, but there was one time that the past tried to come back, when someone tried to break the silence. I was forgetting this and I should tell you that a man came here from London, a doctor, about ten years ago. He was writing a book about children in the war. He asked if he could talk to me about my experiences. He wanted to speak to children who were not Jewish, to get the other side also. I said I would talk to him. I told the doctor to come. But when he sat here with his recorder and his video tape, I was ashamed. It was impossible to speak anything about it. Kurt thought she was going to cry, and he put his hand over hers and felt it tremble. She smiled at him. The doctor, he told me we were child victims, child survivors and our stories hadn't been told and it was important to tell them. I'd never thought of myself that way, she said fiercely. And I didn't want to. I didn't like this word, victim, for myself. I didn't like this word, survivor, for myself. I did not want to be in his book. She stopped and looked at Kurt with some anxiety, Tell me now, please, so I don't make a mistake, what it is that you want to know? I don't want to tell you what you don't want to know.

Please, he said, don't feel you have to do this.

It is why you have come. Who else can help you? If I speak, maybe you will remember. But, please, let us stay with things about your mother and father. This will be eas-

94

ier for me. Kurt nodded, of course, that's what I want to know. The atmosphere had lifted and he was able to ask her, Is my father still alive? Can you tell me about him? Anything you remember?

I knew him, she said, ja, but not well. We were in the same refugee camp with him, in the American Sector. He came later than us. It was in October, about five months after the war ended. That's where your mother met him. He was thirteen years older than we were. He'd been in the Luftwaffe, he was a bomber pilot, and he'd been decorated, also he'd been shot down twice and his legs were injured. He'd been in a military hospital and he'd been a prisoner of war. He had serious fire damage. She stopped abruptly. I too, she said, raising her hands, have fire damage. He stared at her palms: her skin had completely melted and no prints remained; the skin was shiny and white, like soft plastic, like the hands of a mannequin. Frieda said, I fell on the road. The asphalt had melted and my hands got stuck in it. With barely a breath, she went on. Your father's name was Wilhelm. You look, she said, tilting her head, a little like him. The eyes perhaps, his were piercing, blue. He was always a little sick, lung damage . . . He suffered . . . but he did not tell it . . . Else heard some of it, but she didn't tell me. There was once a time when we'd told each other everything, but after it happened . . . The phrase startled him. It began to repeat in his mind . . . After Dresden she didn't speak. That's why I made her write it down.

She wouldn't have done it, he said, not from the way you describe her, if she hadn't wanted to.

Ah. Frieda smiled. She did what had to be done. That was the way we were. She was that way with Wilhelm. She took care of him from the beginning; she'd learned a few things from her work in a clinic, and she was sorry for him.

In America he got a little better, he had surgeries on his legs to help him walk without limping, but there was something in him that didn't mend. He was able to make a good living as an engineer and he worked hard and provided for you both very well. It was when you were a young man, about twenty-four, I think, that he died. She looked at Kurt, eyes wide, and then put her hand to her mouth. You don't remember? I am so sorry. You see, I had forgotten that you don't remember. Shall I stop now? This is a shock, ja?

No, please, go on.

She peered at him a moment and then continued. Your mother came here to tell me he had died. You don't remember anything of this? Ah, I see. I'm so sorry to have to tell you. Do you remember him at all?

Not really. I've a feeling I didn't like him much. I had a dream not long ago that he was standing at a window watching me play with a bomber plane, a British one. In my dream he watched me playing with this plane, it was a Lancaster. But I never knew he was a pilot, knew nothing about any of that. I don't think I've forgotten, I just think it was never talked about, so I never knew it to forget it. But when you said that, about him being a pilot, I remembered that he kept models of English and American war planes in the basement of our home. It seems peculiar that a pilot would keep a collection of enemy planes.

Wilhelm was that way, she said. Perhaps you could call it peculiar. We were all peculiar after the war. He was always comparing the British and American fighter planes with the German ones, as if trying to understand something. He had so many books about planes, about how advanced the technology was by the end of the war. Your mother said he was obsessed with the things he collected.

And, ja, they were from the American and British side: books and model planes, war memorabilia, goggles, leather helmets, even the uniforms . . . Kurt's father appeared in the shadows of the basement wearing a pilot's jacket riddled with bullet holes. He was tall, standing to attention, staring fixedly ahead . . . Frieda was looking down. As soon as Wilhelm died, Else threw everything out – even his medals. She told me she thought he was tired of being alive, that for him things had only got harder, not easier, with time. I myself believe that to be so. Her voice slowed. There was that man who threw himself down the stairwell – the writer, do you remember? Well, the year your father died he didn't have his pneumonia treated. Every year he got it, but that year he wouldn't see a doctor. He was dead by the winter. Your mother was stoic about it. His mother appeared for a moment, standing in the kitchen, holding a small box with an Iron Cross laid on velvet. She closed it. He heard the snap. He saw her foot pressing down the pedal of the trash bin, the lid springing back, the black box sinking beneath coffee grounds and eggshells, the carcass of a chicken. Frieda frowned. Else did not grieve, she just went on without him. She took a breath. Do you remember any of this?

In a way, he said. I haven't forgotten. It's just that there are holes in my memory. I don't remember my parents, but I have a feel for them and sometimes images come up, like an impression in the mind. When you describe my mother, I remember that hardness, that just going on without grieving. It's familiar. And I wonder about that – it makes me wonder about her, about me – all sorts of things half lost and half there.

I think I can understand, Frieda said. She was struggling for words. It is important to remember, she said, if we are to survive, if we have survived, it's important to remember. I know that now. And that doctor, perhaps he was right and I should have spoken for the others who could not . . . But now, what is the point of saying one thing and not another? He nodded. She leaned back in her chair. I hope I don't hurt you with anything I say. Stop me if I do. She looked away. Because after you were born, those first years, for your mother, were very bad years. She came on your first birthday and it was always the same when she came: she gave you to me and I took you. Already I had made the bed, and she went into the bed. She stayed there for several days. The curtains had to be closed just so. No one could come in. She did not eat. She did not speak. And it was for me to look after you while she slept. I had my children; they were a lot older than you, so we all took care of you while she slept. She was not so young then. She'd waited a long time to have you; she was forty-one when you were born. It had been a hard decision for her to have a child, and when you were little it was as if she was afraid of you. She peered at him anxiously. Is it okay I say these things? He nodded, smiled, his heart pierced with sorrow. It's okay, he said. When Else was with me, Frieda said, my husband understood that it was just the two of us. He gave me to her and I waited for her to come out of it. She did not explain. I did not ask. Once she told me she was afraid she might hurt you. Kurt looked up and Frieda took his hand. I don't know what she meant. She only said it one time, the first year she came. She was like a plate that had been dropped.

This must be painful for you, Frieda said, moving her hand to touch his arm. He wondered if she could feel anything with her hands, and then tried to imagine how it might be not to feel pain or pleasure, hot or cold, the textures of food or cloth, Hannah's skin or hair. Kurt, she said, you must understand, I'm not saying she was a bad mother. Not so. She was devoted to you, over-protective, ja, always getting up in a fright, saying, Where is Kurt? Where is he? But very affectionate, kiss, kiss, kiss. She carried you all the time, held you and cuddled you. I had to tell her to let you walk, I had to say, put him down, let him walk. She didn't like you to play with other children; she wanted you to stay with her, as if she was afraid of what might happen to you if she left you. Frieda said, You were not permitted a friend. Loneliness flooded him. He saw himself standing in the corner of a school-yard, watching other children play and not knowing how to. Counting to a hundred and back again, making order with numbers, repeating his times tables over and over. Eating alone in the lunch-room or sometimes with a teacher and finding it hard to speak the way other children did. I knew, Frieda said, that Else could have only one child. Her voice stalled for a second. She had a brother, Rudy, much younger, who was lost in the war.

Frieda sat up in her chair and her voice became stronger. I think also she protected you from your father. What she said about him sometimes made me think this, but I'm not certain. Understand, please. Of some things I am sure, others not. This I know: you were everything to her, but those early years of your life were full of terror for her, and understand, though it was many years after the war, it was with her like yesterday. She'd come, she'd walk in and the minute I opened the door, she'd push you at me and I'd take you from her. After three days she was all right. When she came out of the bed, she would bathe, put on new clothes and then she could walk to me, kiss me and say, Danke.

Frieda stopped and looked at him. What is it? You are looking so sad.

I can't seem to ask.

So. She was quiet a long time. It will be me, she said, who will ask the question for you. Ja?

What question?

She hesitated. You want to know if your mother is still alive? The minute the words were out, Frieda's face divided: her eyes grew wide and frightened while the lower part of her face was composed, and the effect was eerie. She said quietly, One year she stopped coming. It was after Wilhelm died. Frieda bit her lip. I tried to find her. I tried a lot. I wrote letters, I telephoned. I even went to New York looking for her, trying to trace her through the last apartment you'd lived in the Lower East Side. She was always wandering, one apartment after the other, she couldn't settle anywhere. But I couldn't find her. Frieda's mouth was trembling and her eyes were filled with tears. Her face was so raw that Kurt couldn't bear to look at her. Ah, she said, with dismay, you don't know. If she's alive or not – you don't know?

No, he said, exhausted, I can't remember.

12

It was late afternoon. Kurt and Frieda were sitting in a back room when Kurt got up and walked over to the sewing machine in the corner. He sat on the chair and pressed his feet down on the treadle. When the sewing machine began to whirr he looked over at Frieda and laughed. He was messing with levers and opening the cavity under the needle, remembering how to re-thread the needle and fill the bobbin. Frieda handed him a remnant of blue linen. Here, do some hemming, she said. I made your mother a dress from this. I remember it, he said. She pulled a chair closer to him and watched him with amusement. Else and I learned as young girls to sew and we taught all our children. You liked to do it. I still use this old machine; I make clothes for my grandchildren, and sometimes a prom or wedding dress for a girl in town. Our fathers, she said, your mother's and mine, had a factory in Germany. They were in the garment trade a long time. We used to go into the sewing rooms and spend time with the machinists. They were rowdy women, full of fun, with white caps on their heads, and they smoked like chimneys. And, she said, once we knew how to sew we began to make our own clothes, cutting patterns from dresses we took apart, or from designs cut out on newspaper. In America we continued with the sewing. We ordered the same sewing machines from a catalogue, ja, this same one, and we'd swap patterns and make clothes for you children. So, she said, surveying his work, you are good. Watching him pounding out a dead straight seam, she said with satisfaction, This you remember.

In the middle of the floor there was an old cardboard box and some photographs of Kurt and his mother that Frieda had dug out. She'd shown him a framed 5-by-7 that she kept beside her bed: a soft sepia print of his mother, who had an oval face, delicate eyebrows, sad, dark eyes and a mass of curls. Kurt stared at his mother a long time, but apart from the hair, which was reminiscent of Hannah's, he didn't really remember her. She must have been eighteen, Frieda said, it was when we were first here, see, it was taken in Manhattan, 1949. Frieda had photos of him sitting with his mother in a hammock, the two of them on a beach somewhere, one with Kurt standing between Frieda and his mother, laughing, and there was a grainy shot of his mother and father with Kurt looking steadfastly at the camera. When he looked closely at it, he stopped, startled, because in the background was a magnolia tree. He looked up at Frieda: I remember that tree, where was it? Frieda laughed. It was out back, you could see it from the kitchen. Ja, it was a magnificent magnolia, but it was cut down many years ago. We had another one to the right, but that also has gone.

There are no other photos? He was peering again at his mother and himself on the beach; he noticed she was holding his hand in a clutchy way – or was it that he remembered the way she held his hand, hurting his fingers? Frieda said, Somewhere, I may have a picture of their wedding. I know she sent me one. They were married in New York, it was 1950, June. There might also be a photo of Else's mother, your grandmother. She died soon after that wedding.

You don't have any photos of the two of you when you were kids?

Frieda stopped and stared at him, and, for the first time, he tried to imagine the end of a life: everything gone, every trace wiped away, nothing to show you'd lived in that house, that street, that city, nothing to show you'd lived at all. He looked at Frieda and saw how tired she was. He thought he should leave. No, she said, stay a bit longer. She walked over to the window and said, That doctor who came . . . at the time I thought of giving him what your mother wrote. That's what I was referring to before – it's in the attic. A clump of pages tied with string. She looked directly at him. I will give it to you. Her face was tender. Would you read it? Yes, he said slowly, I would. She nodded. I like it that you wait before you speak. She was that way. Let's go downstairs into the kitchen. It's easier there. Less dark. And there's chicken and barley soup which is good. I'll tell you about how we left Germany

So they took up their earlier positions round the table, had some soup, dark bread and cheese, talked of small things in her life – the library where she worked on Tuesdays, the hospital where she did volunteer work on Fridays – where her children were – things that came out easily and left no echo. When she was ready, she told him so, and he listened, interrupting as little as he could.

When, she said, we got out of Dresden, it was '45, before Easter. Spring came early that year. She looked at him steadily – like now, exactly. Do you see how your mother came with you in the middle of February, and that you have come at the same time? She smiled. We are like birds, we know when it's time to go back. This was the time of year that Dresden was destroyed, February 13th was the first day of the bombing, then for two more days, night and day, we were bombed until there was nothing left.

Dresden was the city where we had lived our lives, my parents and all of us were born there, as were your mother's family, many generations. Our houses were close together in the old part of the city, tight together, so you could hear if someone turned in the bed next door, or a baby cried in the early hours of morning. It was a very beautiful city, medieval, everything built tight together, the buildings, the churches . . . and, her voice flared up . . . I must tell you that there was no military reason to bomb it, it was full only of civilians and refugees from the East, it was a hospital city for wounded soldiers – there was no reason to bomb it. I heard this last year for the first time on the television. I could not stop watching, I thought my heart would break when I heard a British voice say that Dresden, what had happened there, was a war crime. It was a military man who said this, he didn't ask to be forgiven, but he took responsibility. I had never heard such a thing, never . . . And I was grateful . . .

She waited, took a breath and then another. When we got out of Dresden, we were taken to the suburbs just outside, some twenty miles, and there we found a little house, empty, undamaged, and we stayed there with our mothers, Else and me, the four of us together. We had not eaten for days, we were filthy and broken-hearted, but it was beautiful there, food on the shelves and sheets on the beds and blankets also, and water in the taps, hot water so we could wash but . . . Well, at first we didn't wash . . . For some reason we stayed in those filthy, burned rags and we did not take them off. I don't know why. It was all that was left . . . and your mother . . . Frieda looked up, startled . . . When she came here, she would sleep in the same clothes and only after she came out of the bed would she put on new ones . . . I hadn't thought it before, but that's what she

104

did, slept in her clothes for three days, not wash, not brush the hair, not eat, and afterward she would change the clothes and begin again.

Frieda, Kurt said, your hands are shaking. Please stop, you're beat. She seemed in a trance. Who knows if I could do this again? You are here. I am here. People can vanish. Her voice cracked, Because, she said, it was in this place, this lovely little villa out of the city, safe in the suburbs, with a garden in blossom, it was here that your mother said to me, I don't want to live any more. Frieda stopped, got up, walked to the windows and looked out. Else was only fourteen, she said softly, I also. She was dangerously unhappy, she could not eat or sleep, sometimes she spent the whole day in the bed and the next and the next. Frieda turned to face him. She did nothing all day. And she did not speak a word. But I knew that, before, she liked to write – poems and diaries – she used to write them every day curled on her bed and she liked to write in different colour inks – all the silly little things that made up our lives, and sometimes she read me parts and we'd sit on the floor and laugh about how we'd been just one year before – so young, so stupid – we would laugh so much. I didn't know what to do to help her, Frieda said, almost defiantly, and her mother, well, she was . . . we all were . . . out of our minds in different ways. Things got very bad. More refugees came, and they'd been through terrible things, and when they spoke of those things Else's hands would shake very badly and she'd run out and I'd be so afraid of what she might do to herself . . . If she saw a small child she would suddenly faint; if someone lit a match to make a fire she would put her hands to her eyes and scream . . . Her mind couldn't stop seeing, but her tongue didn't work.

Frieda's voice speeded up so each sentence came out

like a shot. Everyone was waiting for the Russians, she said, and we were terrified. Everyone was on the run because the war would soon be over. Terrible things would happen to us, we knew this. We couldn't move or make a decision, to go or stay, we just did what had to be done, to stay alive, to keep breathing, one foot in front of the other. A young man committed suicide there. Blew his brains out. We buried him with his shirt wrapped round his head. We did not know who he was, only that he'd come from the East and was trying to find his family. There were others who killed themselves. We found them hanging and cut them down. There was a place to put the dead bodies behind a wall close to the rubbish dump. People came and then disappeared overnight. She put her hands to her head. We were all . . . all of us not clear in our mind . . . It was so unreal . . . so terrible . . . Then, she said, stopping for breath. Things settled a bit. I'm sorry if I confuse you going back and forth, but it comes back to me that way. The weather became warm, and people began to sleep in the garden and there was more space in the house. We tried to find order there: we began to make a family out of the broken pieces. We shared food, made rules about behaviour, took turns with everything, helped each other out. Everybody seemed good again, kind again, like people used to be. Vegetables were growing in the fields, and we had some chickens, eggs, a few pigs. It was better, and it was at this time I said to Else, Write it down. She looked at me like she wanted to hit me. She took up a pencil and wrote down: It's crawling all over my brain, like maggots, all those pictures, everything burning. I want to put a bullet in my head to make it stop.

I made a space for her on the table. I got paper out of the cupboard in the dining room, I found ink and a pen, and I said, Write, Else, let it come out of your brain. Once she began, she couldn't stop, every time I looked in there, she was writing furiously and she would go on night and day, one hand twisting her hair round and round at the back and the other on the paper, scribbling without stopping, her hand shaking, black ink racing across the page. Then she would stop for a day or two, she'd sleep and sometimes she'd scream in broad daylight, and other times I'd have to hold her down so she wouldn't run out. Then she'd go back into the dining room and sit down, take another page and go on writing. When it was done, she pushed it at me and said, Take it. And I took it with me when we left.

Did you read it?

Frieda's face fell. No, she whispered. I'm ashamed to say I did not. I did not have her courage. She looked up. You will be the first person.

We couldn't stay, Frieda said in a dull, flat voice, in the house any longer. Things were breaking down again. We knew the signs. People were stealing. The guns came back. People had knives. No one gave a smile. We looked at each other with suspicion, and we hated the new ones when they came because we didn't have enough for ourselves to give to them also. We started walking again toward Dresden. There was nothing else to do. The roads were jammed with refugees, and with the Soviet army, jeeps and trucks full of soldiers, and there were slave labourers trying to get home – one stream went west, the other east. Her face lifted for a moment with a smile. Do you know what I remember now? she said. An American soldier who was walking past us on the road, and he stopped and looked at Else and me, and slowly he took out a pack of gum and handed us each a piece. Frieda's eyes closed for a moment.

I will never forget how he smelt, that American, how clean, with his chewing gum and his new uniform, how sweet and undamaged and alive he was. I'd not smelt anything like that for so long, or tasted anything sharp or scented like that for so many years. When he smiled his teeth were white and I thought he'd come from heaven. There were people who were walking skeletons with huge eyes and twigs for limbs and they didn't look up and if they fell they were stepped over. If a plane came overhead we jumped into ditches or ran across the fields to the trees. If a child had no one to carry her, she'd be left behind. Sometimes you saw a mother sitting with a dead baby or a family lying dead together and if they had something we wanted we took it. Once I took a piece of bread from a dying child, I snatched it from her hand as she was slumped over and I was terrified that she might suddenly lift her head or grab at me to get it back. I saw two men fighting over a piece of dog. The mass graves were on the outskirts of the city with piles of dead bodies all around, but there was no one to bury them. We had to walk through it all and the smell was terrible. We wore filthy clothes and put mud and animal shit on our faces to keep the Russian soldiers off us, but all the same they came and took us and in front of everyone, taking turns, one after the other.

Frieda shook herself free. It was while we were staying in a refugee camp outside Dresden, she said, that we heard on the radio that Germany had surrendered. It was May 8th. None of us felt anything. We didn't speak about it and after that we stopped listening to the radio. We thought of little things, food, water, that was it, we held onto each other, if someone was lost we would find them right away. If I left, Else followed me, if her mother went outside, Else followed her. We were terrified of losing one another, of being alone in the world. All we could do was walk, lines and lines of us, some with a tied bag, others a broken suitcase, some with nothing at all. And with the end of the war new terrors came. We kept moving, but we kept close together because we needed to be near other people, we were terrified of dying alone, or being picked off, one by one. We walked huddled close together, day after day, foraging for food in the fields, digging in the ground if we saw broken things, gathering wood to make fires in the shelter of the ruins. And we kept on walking. We were silent as we walked. No one looked at the other. If we came upon other refugees no one spoke to them or looked at them. We hated the refugees because we were like them. We were all filthy and starving and desperate and willing to steal, to take the boots off the old man, to hide bread, to push the young girl at the soldier. We began to hate everyone. We'd become barbarians. This is what the roads and the wandering did to us. At the house it had been different, we were people then, but we didn't think of those days because they were over. And so it went, always walking, always moving on until much later we managed to get to Gera and behind the American lines and after that things changed again. And there we stopped.

13

Frieda and Kurt sat together a long time in the twilight, not speaking, until, finally, he got up, kissed her on the cheek and left the kitchen. He walked slowly down the hallway and when he got to the front door he came to a stop. He stood absolutely still. And then he straightened his back and turned the way a soldier turns and walked back into the kitchen. He saw Frieda sitting where he'd left her, staring out of the window. He walked up, crouched in front of her and rested his hands on her knees. She's dead, isn't she? My mother. She's dead. He was looking into her eyes with desperation and hope, his mouth slightly open. Frieda put her hands on either side of his face and held him. Ja, she whispered, she is dead. She leaned forward and grabbed him and held him against her as the muscles in his back went into spasm. For a while that's all he felt. He tried to pull away but she hung on to him. Cold crept all the way up his arms and across his shoulders, his hands went numb. He got up and left.

He went back to the motel and lay on the bed, staring into the dark for a long time, waiting for something to break. He heard the cars on the highway outside and then nothing. Shock moved down his limbs and settled in his feet. His body was nothing more than a weight, inanimate and dead. He got under the covers and fell into a deep sleep. When he woke it was to a loud, shrill sound and, as he frantically disentangled himself from the sheet, he stared at the phone. He couldn't pick it up. It was dark inside; headlights illuminated the highway and a flare shot through the curtains and crossed the floor. The heavy rumble of trucks intercepted the soft roar of cars and was followed by long stretches of silence. When the phone rang again he yanked it off the receiver. He heard Hannah's voice but couldn't speak.

Kurt?

He could hear her breathing but not his own.

Kurt? Are you okay? Her voice was tender.

He began to sob in a deep, wrenching way. He put his hand over his mouth and eyes, his body doubled up. After a long silence, she said, Kurt? What happened?

Too much to tell.

Just breathe, she said, waiting, just breathe.

My mother, he said, stoically, is dead.

I'm so sorry, she said, repeating the words, Oh, Kurt, I'm so very sorry.

He could see his mother walking up a hill and turning back to pull him up the rocks and then grabbing him and holding him so tightly he could barely breathe. Standing in front of him as he sat on the kitchen table while she bandaged his knee; he was wearing leather shorts and the seam cut into his thigh, and she said, I told you not to go there, I said you mustn't play on the road. It was summertime and she'd filled up a plastic pool and was pouring water over his head from a red bucket. She was standing behind him while he blew out five candles. They'd walk in the snow and she'd go first so he could step into her footprints . . . Fire engines scared her half to death. She loved Lindt chocolate. She'd sit for hours with the cat on her lap, stroking the fur, until she fell asleep. If he made her angry or hurt her she'd not speak for days. Then she'd blow up.

He put down the phone, sat on the edge of the bed and sobbed. When he retrieved the phone Hannah was still there. Do you want me to call back later? No, I need to tell you. I'm afraid I'll forget. You won't forget. Her voice was calm and he attached himself to it. Get back in the bed, she said, your teeth are chattering. He climbed in and, as the panic subsided, he found he could talk again.

He began to tell her what Frieda had told him. She listened. If she spoke at all, her voice was soft and after a while Frieda's story came pouring out of him. It seemed to him she understood about Frieda, his mother, his father, the walking out of Dresden, the end of the war. He told her everything he could, and what he said to her over and over was, I didn't know any of this. I've never read anything about it, not this side of it. Why didn't we *know*? Why's it been so hidden? After a while, some of his own life drifted back and he could tell her memories of his school days, a house in New York State where there were mountains, a summer house by the sea, his parents in a room with blue walls, a kitchen filled with silence and tension. Times of playing alone in a basement, running with a bomber plane held high in his hand, near a pond with goldfish in it, and how he'd tripped and the plane had crashed and sunk in the pond. He could see himself wading into the water and slime and pulling it out to see the paint on the roundels, blue and red circles, melting. He'd run to the end of the yard and buried it, and lived in terror for days, waiting for his father to find him.

He remembered that his mother had talked to him when they were sewing together. Thing is, he said to Hannah, Frieda kept saying that no one spoke about anything to do with the war or the bombing of Dresden, that she didn't, that my mother didn't. But my mother out of the blue would come out with these odd, broken sentences about Dresden, leaving Dresden, walking back into Dresden – random images that seemed to surface briefly before she shut them off. If I asked her a question or my dad came in she'd clam up. But some of the things Frieda told me I already knew, or while Frieda was speaking I'd suddenly remember them as if they'd been waiting in my mind all along like a memory loop joining up, suddenly I'd see the whole thing. I remember the model planes in the basement clearly now, especially the smaller American planes – the Mosquitoes and Thunderbirds – how beautifully they were made. He kept them under glass like butterflies. Once I caught him down there wearing the full regalia of a British fighter pilot. We stared at one another, he and I – I was about eight – and, without clicking his heels, he lifted his hand in a quiet, elegant gesture and touched his forehead the way the Brits do in the movies. He told me to salute. And I did.

But something happened and my mother stopped telling me things. I get the sense that my father saw me sewing with her one day and kind of lost it. All I can get is his anger and my fear and my mother running at me when he ripped the material out of my hands. He began to yell at her and I got up . . . and he picked me up and threw me against the wall. She became hysterical and since she was always very quiet it was terrifying to see her like that. She screamed at him in German, words I didn't understand. Then the silence returned. That's how it was. There was a whole lot of silence in that house and a whole lot of crazy stuff that started and stopped and it feels very confused in my mind: I only get a piece of it and then it's gone.

When he'd finished talking he was exhausted again. You talk to me, he said. Tell me what you've been doing. She said she'd been looking into some things about memory, going back into her psych books, going on the web, talking to colleagues. Listening to her he thought she knew more than she was telling him or that she suspected things and didn't want to say. He became quiet, suspicious. What are you trying to tell me, Hannah?

Just what I'm learning myself, she said. Memory is so complicated, especially traumatic memory. Maybe you have some kind of dissociated memory and it's lifting, but it's hard to say how much you'll get back, or when. I just think you might need some help. And I hope you don't mind, but I've been looking for someone you might consider talking to . . .

A shrink?

An expert on memory, about how it works, different kinds of memory, things that are eerie and strange – like the kids in Texas who's parents were Nazis. When I spoke to Erich he said maybe some of the past has slipped over into the present, and that you might be carrying your mother's history. Kurt was silent a long time. Would you, Hannah asked, be able to talk about this to someone? No? Well, perhaps not right now. I understand. But, will you at least think about meeting him? And would you like me to come to Dresden? He thought if he saw her he'd go off like a bomb, if she touched him he'd disintegrate. No, he said, don't come, not yet. What can I do? Stay close, he said, I need to hear your voice. He was aware how much he needed her, how she steadied and righted him, and the dependence felt a little dangerous. Like a refugee, he needed to stay with other people, not wanting to be out there alone, to be picked off one by one, to die alone. I'll leave my phone on, she said, call day or night, anytime. I'll pick up. I'm going to stay here a bit longer, he said. I need to go back to Frieda now, make sure she's okay, that we're both okay. Are you okay, Hannah?

I'm fine. Don't worry about me.

Are you telling the truth?

Absolutely

He hesitated. Frieda, he said, gave me something my mother wrote. And before I left today, she gave it to me. It's a stack of papers, a record of some kind that she wrote soon after the fire-bombings.

Are you going to read it?

Yes.

Well, perhaps, she said, take a little at a time. Not to be overwhelmed. Her voice cracked. You've been through too much.

When he put the phone down and the room was silent he wished he'd asked her to come. The isolation was unbearable. His mother was dead. He had no mother. He felt so lonely. He saw her running with him on a beach, and turning back, and bending down to grab his hand. He saw her trying to help him with his homework, he heard her voice with its broken English. It's a language I'm afraid of, she'd say, biting her lip. And he'd say quickly, It's okay. I can do it myself. And once she'd said, I used to like to write. And with that, like a blast of heat, he was overwhelmed with such love, such love and such pain and gratitude all at the same time that he could scarcely bear it. He picked up the yellowed sheets of paper tied securely with string, and put them down again. He looked at the words in beautifully formed German script: *Dresden, Germany, 1945, Else Altmann, 14 jahren.* For a split second the edges of the papers caught fire.

Frieda. Okay, I give up. I'll do it. When you told me how your hands were pulled out of the burning road and your handprints were left behind, then I knew I must do it. I don't know where to start but not at the end. I have to do things in order. I was the one with the neat room. You the one with the dead apples under the bed. And I'm doing this only because I love you and because you're the only one who knows me the way I was before it happened. You cried when you asked. You got down on your knees and made me the altar. Frieda, I'll try it, but if I can't I can't. If I stop I stop. I'm scared if I begin I'll burn. I must start by going back to when we were children and everything was still there. Now, everything is gone and I don't know how that can be and we can still be here. It's impossible to believe. I can't take it in, so I have to go to when I can remember, to the time we were babies and sat in the tub naked and fat and smiling, the way we were in those photos that Mother kept in a big box in the attic, where we had ribbons sticking out of our hair, and we squatted on the lawn with our knees up showing our underpants and you had on your mother's pearls. Our mothers were close as houses and they'd be sitting on chairs smoking and watching to make sure we didn't drown, first in the tub and later on in the cement pool that got so many cracks it had to be buried. But that was later. In the time I'm in now they'd be dangling their legs in the water, splashing each other with their toes. When a tune came on the radio they'd get up and dance, swirling and throwing their heads back until Mother would stop dramatically because she'd remember Rudi was taking his nap inside and might be crying. She couldn't bear for him to cry. When he was first born that seriously got on my nerves because she gave me the shove when he came. She denied that but she did. She'd waited a long time for him and there were thirteen years between the two of us and that's a lot, but I felt bad about not being her baby-girl any more. And when I saw him in the cot I wanted to whack him. But how could I have? I can't believe I thought that and it makes me feel evil as a snake.

I thought just now to stop. I was too scared. But then I think about your hands in the bandages and the smell. And I'll try again. I must be as brave as you because, I'm older, three months. And I feel even older now though really we're still both fourteen. I used to tell myself I was more mature because I had that small experience with Hans, not a big experience, just kissing and not even the kind of kissing I know is not nice, just kissing with the mouth closed which is okay. Hans already had hair on his face so his cheeks were like sandpaper and it hurt when he kissed, and when he began the rubbing I knew that had to stop and I slapped his hand and that started the trouble. He wouldn't talk to me after that. He used to come over to Willi's next door to throw the ball up into the net and the thump, thump, thump of the ball going up and down against the wall would drive me nuts. Hans did it to annoy me because of me hitting his hand. He started to pretend to really like that swampy girl, Helge, running after her bike and then when she sped off he'd throw up his hands and yell while you and I sniggered and went inside to try and find the last little piece of chocolate or milk Mother was saving for Rudi when he'd be screaming his head off. We never did find them because she made damn sure we didn't. That's what I mean about Rudi getting stuff I didn't.

Things were easy then. Time moved very slowly until the war came and then it speeded up even though everything else had stopped. It was so long since we'd had new clothes that fit properly and felt nice to wear, everything had got thin with washing and was tight and the wool had got hard. We were thinner too and your boobs got smaller but you had always much more than a handful so it was okay for you. Food wasn't easy to get unless you took a train to the country, but the trains were slow and later the farm people wouldn't let us have any. Do you remember how we saw that man steal eggs? And then someone else took bread, and then it got to be okay to steal and we did it and it was normal and it was fun. But the stealing stopped because what's to steal when there's nothing left? It was a long time since we'd come back with a bit of ham, and of course forget about meat or a piece of sausage, but we were lucky because we had the bees so at least when there was only the hard black bread we could put honey on it and let it soak in and stick our fingers in and suck on them and that was the greatest thing because nothing tasted of anything by then.

The thing that was really bad was Father. You told me not to worry about him but you knew. We'd see him with the old man next door, both standing in the frames of their doors with their felt hats on, saying how bad it was getting, worse every day, bad, bad, bad. They spoke every hour of every day about the war, as if the world had stopped, but as time went by they talked about it less and then stopped listening to the radio also. We used to laugh at them behind their backs – what was the matter with them about the war? We were safe at home then, nothing had happened. Your dad and mine owned the factory but of course they weren't making the fancy sleeping clothes any more, the silk pyjamas and gowns you could see right through. I remember when the girls in the store used to wrap up the nightclothes in long white boxes filled with blue tissue and when you took out a nightgown it was so beautiful you couldn't bear to scrumple it up by sleeping in it. When I was twelve I got some pale pink pyjamas with white piping round the edges and I looked at them for three days before I put them on. But that was before we'd started sleeping in our clothes because of having to get up when the sirens went off and go down into the cellar. It was freezing down there and you came to mine because it was drier usually, but not always.

* * *

When I think back to then, the war wasn't a horrible thing for you and me because our lives went on pretty nicely, and we weren't changed the way some people were, like Father, who was getting bent out of shape by all he had to put up with at the factory. But for a long while he didn't tell any of this to us, so we just went on as usual. Of course it was boring to have to stand in those long lines for bread, but we didn't care, and we didn't even mind going to the church halls where they were selling old clothes dirt cheap. We could scrabble through the piles of stuff and look at the silk brassieres and slinky dresses from way back when, and there were glamorous things too thrown in with the thick sweaters that everyone wanted. Once we found a red lipstick in the pocket of a velvet jacket. I gave it to Mother since I wasn't allowed to wear lipstick. There were black lace dresses, tight at the waist with a low neck and organdy ruffles to show off the boobs. And the excitement of finding shoes with heels and once also curlers to make waves in the hair.

But for Mother the old clothes were disgusting and she'd stand there with her arms crossed and refuse to touch them, and when I brought her my pile of clothes she'd stand back as if they smelled. Well, of course they smelled, but you could wash them and put them on the line. She wouldn't buy anything for precious Rudi from there – because she said he shouldn't wear clothing we didn't know who'd worn before. Just think, it could be something a refugee had worn and was full of lice and disease. Those refugees that came in on the freight trains from Silesia there was no way anything they were wearing could be put up for sale. Anyway, they weren't allowed in the church halls. I never saw any lice in what I got, but of course I washed it with that hard soap that smells pretty vile but which is all we had, not even a name on it, just a yellow block cut up like cheese that you got once a month. Mother has a way of seeing things worse than what they are and it doesn't help now any more than it ever did.

119

* * *

Things were exciting for us that weren't for the grown-ups. The sirens going off all the time didn't bother us and sometimes we didn't go down to the cellar because nothing ever happened, just the sirens and the wardens rushing around and then an hour or so later the All Clear. We'd be down there giggling and bored, annoying people by goose-stepping with our arms up until the warders banged on the door and we could come up again. School was still going, but we had to use both sides of the paper and pencils were down to stubs. There weren't enough teachers but that was good too. We had to bring our own lunch and the very poor kids looked at our food so hard we had to give them some. That made us feel like angels of mercy. Our uniforms, the purple and pale blue and the edge of gold, well the skirts were halfway up our thighs. We had to take the seams and hems out, but since everyone looked a fright, it didn't matter. You got a really long one from somewhere and sewed the skirt into fish tails and said you were going to a dance. And the two of us danced, do you remember, in the dining room when they pushed the chairs and tables back after lunch. No one bothered about what you wore, or the holes in the shoes or the colours. And I always had you and you always had me and we could tell each other everything.

I even told you father had a visit from the Gestapo even though I'd sworn on the Bible not to tell a living soul. I was scared to death they'd come to take him away, but we weren't hiding anyone. After they left he went to his room for two days and wouldn't come out. Things changed at the factory in a big way after that, which was a shame because we used once to go there a lot. You and me we'd take a tram to the factory pretty much every week. Your dad had gone to war but mine hadn't because of the leg that had got damaged in the accident. So of course my dad was managing things by himself and that wasn't easy because it was a big factory with a lot of responsibility. When the Gestapo came it was to tell Father to change the factory into making other kinds of clothing. The Gestapo were going to take over the factory and a day later they did it. They made Father stay to keep things running smoothly but he wasn't giving the orders any more. What they were making in there was uniforms for Jews to wear in the camps and it was Jews that were making the uniforms. The uniforms were white with wide dark stripes, and they were like the pyjamas that the factory once made, in the shape at least. The prison camps were punishment for Jews because they were the reason our country had gone to the dogs before the Führer took over and turned the economy around and made us proud to be Germans again. This is what Father used to say, until the Gestapo came.

They brought the prisoners from the camp in truckloads in the middle of the night and they stayed somewhere close to the factory, it was all kept secret but we knew, though we didn't know exactly what was going on inside the factory because the guards were all Gestapo and the old guards, even old Schmitty, went. Father's other employees were sent to war, unless they were really old and sick, anyone else just vanished. And there was that day when we heard something horrible had happened outside the factory and we wanted to see. Outside the gates we saw the body of a girl just a few years older than us and she had bullets in her back. All the blood had leaked out. I didn't know a body had so much blood. Flies were stuck in it. They left her out there for a few days so we could get the message. I had a bad time with what they'd done to her hair and I couldn't get it out of my mind and I was glad that we weren't allowed to get too close because it was sad the way her skirt kept blowing up in the wind and she couldn't pull it down to hide herself. After they took the factory Father was no longer the father I'd loved, the one who used to play games and take me hiking and who once when Mother was in hospital having Rudi and I was unhappy said, You can tell me all

121

the bad things you've ever done and I'll never ask you about them again. That was the greatest day: all my sins flying out the window and never coming back again.

Father was silent all the time, suddenly no jokes and no teasing. It was because he was allowed to do nothing but show the prisoners how to work the machines, and when the machines broke down he wasn't allowed to have his own mechanics fix them. Everything had to be done by the Gestapo. The clothes being made inside were all one size and with a string around the waist and no hemming because the camp people didn't deserve that. Father was offended by the way things were being done in the factory because he was particular about his supplies, and the quality, and now material was coming in that wasn't fit for clothes – junk cloth that jammed up the machines and made the cloth buckle and tear and made dust and was too rough to turn into a decent garment. And he objected to the dogs they had in there to make people work and also they'd smashed the whole heating system, because the Jews didn't need heating since their blood was different from ours, so Father was sick with everyone else because it was freezing. I know there were other things he didn't tell, not even to Mother, but he was very dark, and at night I heard him pacing up and down in the room above mine. But we didn't ask him because we knew he couldn't say.

Before they took the factory, I used to go there all the time. I'd sit in Father's chair in his cozy office with samples of wool and flannel and silk and satin all displayed so you could feel them, and written on the back it told you how many threads in each and I liked it when Father would teach me about fabrics. One of the machinists taught me and you how to sew till we could whiz up and down the seams really fast, racing each other. Father gave me an old machine to take home and do you remember how we start-

ed making skirts out of any old rag? The blonde secretary from Dusseldorf called Lotte brought me hot chocolate in Father's office and sometimes a piece of cake. That was another girl's life.

Anyway, in spite of Father's unhappiness and the factory gone, it really wasn't bad, not for us. It was exciting at night to go out and look for boys even though we weren't allowed to we still went, but soon of course the boys started going off to be trained as soldiers and we'd stand and watch them parading back and forth, proud and idiotic as they were, always so full of themselves. But in a day they were turned into something that wasn't a boy any more. They walked stiffly in those uniforms and their faces were like rocks, but at least they had thick coats, unlike the rest of us with our elbows sticking through patches, though I noticed their coats weren't new, nor the boots, but they didn't care. They jumped up on the back of those trucks with their guns and helmets and they sang about killing the English and the Allies and of making a hole in the earth for dead Ivans to fall into. Those boys – I mean, imagine, boys like Hans and Pieter, thick as cowshit – they were being glorified as the boy defenders of the Third Reich and their job was to turn the war around. How dumb could that be?

The truth is we were scared shitless of the Red Army, not the war, just the Red Army. We'd heard horrible stories but I don't want to remember that. I'm not sure there's any use in remembering anything. I'm not even sure why I agreed to do this, and perhaps it's only because while you think I'm writing about what happened, I'm remembering before – such a sad word, like the other sad words that stick in my mind . . . If only, if only, if only . . . When the boy soldiers had finished their strutting and pushing up their arms and clicking their heels, they climbed up on the back of the trucks and started to pull away down the street. Your brother Jurgen was on the back, and you ran after the truck, you

*ran and ran and your body in your dark dress was getting small-
er as I watched you run, but not one, not one of those boys we'd
known all our lives looked at you, not once, not even your brother.
And it surprised me because of your boobs and they moved a lot
inside your dress when you were running, but none of those boys
who before were always banging into you and ogling and touching, not one of them would look at you from that truck. I knew
then they weren't boys any more. When I caught up with you,
you'd bent over with your head hanging down and your hands
on your knees because you must have been exhausted from running that way.*

*After that we went wild. We wanted to take risks like the boys
going to war and it didn't matter what happened to us any more.
The waiting for the end was becoming horrible. And I didn't
want to be home because Mother was getting peculiar, cleaning
the windows all the time and jumping each time there was a
knock on the door and once I saw her curling some strands of her
hair round and round her finger and pulling it out. Home was
getting horrible. And that's when we started to break into some
of the locked-up empty houses with notices on the door not to
trespass or be shot. Well, who was there to shoot us who knew us
and so would? You didn't want to do it but I made you. We got
in the back through the cellar door, and once we broke a window
and were so terrified that we ran and threw ourselves in the long
grass in case we were shot in the back. Those houses were all
built tight together and all of them were empty so you didn't
have to worry about a neighbour reporting you. Once there'd
been people living in them. We knew some of the people in those
houses and once I went to a party there. Then they started to disappear until one day they'd all gone. No one spoke about it and
no one dared to go near those houses. Except you and me because
we'd had it with everything by then and we wanted to be anar-*

chists, we knew that word from school and it seemed like a good thing to be when everything was falling to pieces and who gave a shit when we could die at any moment just like that. So all the time we were running on the streets, taking messages, delivering things back and forth for people because mail and all that wasn't happening any more and sometimes we got a piece of food out of it.

But the houses were what really fascinated us, they were forbidden houses, and mysterious because no one could remember people leaving from them – suddenly they were empty and the notices slapped on the doors. When you looked through a window after shifting a plank some of the insides were completely empty, but others had furniture in the right place, chairs around a dining room table, curtains and rugs, armchairs by the fireplace and all that, and sometimes it looked as though the owners had left in a great hurry because there were papers all over the floor, and jewellery boxes tipped out with unfortunately nothing in them, and suitcases half-filled and then left open on the floor. We managed to get into one of the houses that still had stuff in it, it took a number of days and we had to go back for tools, but we got in through the cellar and broke open the door into the kitchen. We were looking for food and there were tins of soup and beans and peas and carrots, jam and rice and tea and coffee, sugar and things like that. We took as much as we could and I had to lie to Mother, she knew I was lying but all she said was, Did anyone see you? I said, Not a chance. She said, Don't go back. D'you hear?

Frieda. I didn't say you could read it and just because I'm writing it for you doesn't make it yours. No. So you've no right to accuse me of not writing about what happened. I can write what I like. I wanted to tell you to do it yourself and to be truthful I wanted to hit you very hard. It was a very scary thought because once I'd never have imagined hitting you, or anyone for that matter, but now I could shoot someone or hit them with something seriously heavy so their heads would split open and their brains fall out. And to think I wanted to hit you, my poor Frieda, who's been in such terrible pain that when you can't take it any more you just fall down on the floor and I have to pour cold water over you and smack your cheeks softly and pray, come back, come back, but of course you don't want to because your burned hands would start up again and we have nothing, not even an aspirin left. The burns are so deep they don't heal and now you walk around with them all soggy and green because the bandages make it worse, but if the wind blows on them you scream blue murder. Don't think because I can't say anything, I don't care. But when I wrote on top of a page YOU DO IT you showed me your hands and said, How can I? I don't think that's fair, Frieda, and I don't think it's nice. I told you I would, but still it took me two days to get to it, but that was because of Mother, having to take care of her in her crying and screaming, it took all my time, but now finally she's sleeping.

Mother was out of the city when the first bombs fell, but even being out in the countryside she could see flames and the sky red with black smoke and for a full night she didn't know if Father and I were alive. She'd left me at school the day she took the train because she wanted to see grandma who was scared. Mother told me to go right home after school to make sure Father had his supper at six and she'd take the train back with Rudi and be home by ten. Well that didn't happen. She couldn't get back because of the bombing and after it happened she couldn't work out in her mind how things had changed so dramatically from the day she took the train to the country and the night of the bombing. She kept getting the days wrong.

When morning came she left grandma and went back to the station to take the first train back into Dresden. The train went some of the way but then it had to stop because the tracks were *sticking up in the air. In the end she had to get a lift from a farmer who was also going in to see what had happened to his family. They didn't know if anyone could be alive after the bombing because it went on and on, first at two in the morning, and then at noon the smaller American planes kept diving low shooting with machine guns into people running away from the fires. All Mother could see was this thick black smoke in the air above Dresden and it seemed not to move at all and they were terrified and not saying a word on that drive going in. When she found me she was a wreck and I really don't know how she found our house at all except it had a piece of it still standing and she said she recognized the wallpaper. I'd been down in the cellar with Father waiting for the All Clear which didn't come and then the bomb hit and after the explosions stopped I looked around but I couldn't see Father because there was so much smoke and I was choking and coughing. I pushed all the plaster and bricks off me and when I was free I wet my underclothes from the bottle and put them over my nose and mouth to stop choking so I could look for Father. At first I couldn't see him at all and I was happy because I thought he'd got out but I knew he wouldn't leave me in there by myself so he must be at the back where the storage cases were. I tried to get over there by climbing over the bricks and glass and rubble but the water pipes had burst so water was gushing out of the walls which was good because it had put out most of the fire but also bad because it made boiling hot steam so my face was burning up and I couldn't blink and it was dangerous to touch anything. I started calling for him in case he'd moved though I knew he wouldn't do that because he'd said we must both stay close to the door so the wardens could let us out after the All Clear. Then I saw that the things from the kitchen were all over the cellar, part of the tiles and the oven door and amongst the rubble I saw a piece of Father, his hand was sticking out and I looked and tried to understand how it had got there,*

127

separate from him like that, but I couldn't put anything together because everything was crazy unreal like dreaming. I tried to lift his hand out but it wouldn't come out so I knew he was still attached to it, buried under there. I started to dig and scrape and haul things off and call, Father, Father, I'm coming. I was so afraid that he was suffocating. I had to force myself to calm down and think. I saw the lid of a steel pot and used it as a shovel and I kept digging down into the rubble but when I found a bit more of him I was afraid of scraping his face. There were chunks of wood and one of the hotplates from the kitchen and all of Mother's good china in pieces and I couldn't move some of the heavy stuff, but I tried to free him by moving him a little and then digging furiously all the way round him. I saw his leg and scraped other stuff off his body until I saw his neck and head, but he was face down in water and I looked and I pulled and pulled at him to get up, get up, but he wouldn't.

I had to get out because in spite of the gushing pipes there were still small fires burning in the corners and smoke kept curling up and I couldn't breathe. Fallen plaster and dust were all over, lumps of stone and brick, but you couldn't look at a piece and say, that's a bit of the music room although there was part of a cupboard crushed flat and a piece of Mother's blue dress mixed up with things from the other end of the house like typewriter keys and Rudi's mug. The stairs were mostly collapsed but the two top ones were still there and I had to throw myself against the door many times until there was enough room so I could start clawing to get enough space to squeeze out. I could barely breathe even when I was out. I looked around me and there was nothing except black cut-out houses the way you have cut-out clothes for dolls. The roofs had their heads blown off and if you looked through all you saw was air. The windows were missing and there was melted glass and a chair or banister or body or cat splattered all over the

128

place and there were two bicycles and a head up in a tree which was Mr Frankel's. I ran to your house and there was nothing on top and when I banged on your cellar door I heard nothing. So I thought you were dead but I also thought you weren't. In another house I heard people screaming down in a cellar where flames were bursting out but I couldn't help them. I walked home again. I saw no one. In the middle of the houses fires were raging and sparks were flying and making new fires and there was a quiet roaring sound that never stopped. There were bits of ash and paper blowing, blowing. And then so very quiet. Like the end of the world.

The roof was blown off our house but the outside walls were still there, three of them, and on the left side where the rose bushes used to be there was some inside wall, enough to make some shelter from the wind that was blowing all the time and very cold and horrible. I would not permit myself to cry because there are some times when crying would be sacrilege. I went back down in the cellar where Father was and when I came back up I got to work. I stuffed debris and cloth and broken bricks into the empty window frames, and propped up the charred door, kicking at the debris and stamping it down. I wished I had a broom so I could tidy up but none of the things in the house were there any more. I'd brought Father's tools from the cellar and a pair of his gloves which helped my hands which were bleeding. And I stayed there in that place I'd made because Father always said, Stay in the place where you were last. Don't go wandering off or no one will find you. He told me this when we went to the fair or a big store where I might get lost. So I stayed in the shelter and waited for a very long time. There was nothing to eat and no pipes for water and I saw no one. The houses with the infernos burning in the middle were still burning, I heard the crackle and soft roar, but those people who'd been screaming weren't screaming any more.

* * *

When Mother found me I was huddled into the wall and she grabbed me and held me against her so hard I had to pull her fingers out of me. Rudi was squashed between us and she was howling because she'd had to walk through such terrible sights to find us and all the time walking she didn't know if she could find the house because how to know one street from another when everything was shattered and fallen down and the streets covered with burnt lumps and burnt cars and furniture and chimney pots and glass. She stood back from me and said, Where's Father? And my mouth stopped and I couldn't. She shook me hard and I said, He's in the cellar and the ceiling fell on top of him and crushed him. She screamed at me, Is he alive or dead? Dead, I said. Just like that I said it. She was about to go down and I grabbed her, Don't go down there, you can't get down the stairs, they've collapsed. But she said in a tiny voice, I have to get him out. I said, I've covered him with pieces of the house and with stones the way they did in ancient times. He's buried. I got every part of him under and made him a decent burial mound. She was sobbing all over Rudi who began to whimper. I said I'd made a cross from two pieces of wood and stuck it on top and asked God to take his soul out of this terrible place if He could find it. And I held Mother and kissed her forehead and rocked her as best I could. Then I had to get us out of there because everything was shaking, and you could hear the buildings falling down, thud, thud, thud. There was some fire at the edges of the cellar that I hadn't been able to stamp out and I was afraid it would get to the coal bunker in there and then whoosh.

I had to take over because Mother wasn't capable. When the factory was taken from us and Father was so bitter Mother got a bit weird, yes, I have to say it, but when Father died she couldn't think straight any more. All she could do was wail and rock and hang onto Rudi. All she could ask was what day was it and was

130

it still Shrove Tuesday? She and Rudi were covered with the ash that was blowing all the time and her clothes were burned where sparks had caught. Her hair was burned where it fell down and you could see the bald patches she'd made from pulling it out that she'd been trying to hide. She had a deep cut on her leg from a piece of broken steel she'd stumbled over. There was no milk for Rudi because she'd used it all up and all the stores had been bombed away. I saw my mother sitting in the devastation of our house and it was beginning to get dark. I said to her, Mother, let's get to the Grosser Garten, it must be where people would go because there are not so many buildings there to burn and I don't want to be alone here. Around us everything was still burning and I was afraid they'd come back and bomb us again. I took Mother's hand and I said, Come with me, I know the way. It's a long walk, but we can get there. Well, I looked at her shoes and of course she'd been walking over the melted roads so her shoes were destroyed. I made her sit down, and I took off my boots and I gave them to her to put on. She complained, but I was strict. I said, Do you want to walk in those things you're wearing over the asphalt and get stuck in it? And we started to walk away from home, Mother looking back as if she thought she must remember the way back. She stopped and asked, Where's Tant Anna and Frieda? I said I didn't know, perhaps you'd gone to another place. I didn't tell her your house was gone because all she'd have to do was just look across and see all the houses were gone, but she didn't. I didn't look back either but in my heart I said goodbye to Father.

I stopped writing for some days because I was sick, but you came when I was better and said, Show where you are, and I wrote: I can't go any further. Leave me alone. You went to look after Mother and left me in the room and I sat a long time looking out through the windows where there are trees and some have small blossom that is pink and white like a wedding. There were no trees left after the planes came, there were just burnt branches sticking into the cold sky and sticks all over the ground that you could have drawn a picture with. On that second day when the sun shone there were no buildings to cast a shadow, and then the rainstorms came and everything began to move and things began to float. We began to walk, Mother and Rudi and I. I'd taken Father's good jacket off him before I put the debris over him to make the burial mound. I put it on Mother to comfort her because it smelled of tobacco. I wanted to wear it myself, but she needed it more. Instead I took his boots and I discovered for the first time what a small man he was. I put his boots on and they fitted me. When we began walking we saw dead people every-where, and children like burnt puppies with their legs all twisted and some were wearing carnival clothes with bits of red and blue and green burned in the skin. By the school, I saw a boy sitting very still on the bench and I went up to him. But even though he looked like he was sleeping he was dead and I didn't understand because the others were black and shrunken and you'd never walk up and think anything but dead, but that boy got stuck in my mind because he was sitting up all right but still dead. Mother said, I don't know if I can any more. I said, We must, for Rudi, we must. Don't look. Just walk. So we dragged on and we were in a trance or dumb or sleepwalking and we saw people in pieces on the street who'd been blown out of their houses . . . And there was also this . . . but never mind. It began to rain again and this was good because it wet our clothes, and though it was freez-ing it was better to have rain keep the sparks from getting into our faces and eyes because I was mortally afraid that we were going to catch fire and end up like the burned people everywhere. To get anywhere you had to step over bodies or kick them out of the way and we did it though I couldn't believe we could we did. And in my mind I was thinking, dead, dead, dead, and I kept say-

ing it and screwing up my eyes not to see. And sometimes you saw a person who was alive or crawling through the rubble and they didn't see us and we didn't see them because we were walking and our eyes were fixed on that. And I thought God must be somewhere in this because He's everywhere and everywhere is God but I couldn't find Him.

Mother seemed to think she could get us back to the main station where there was a shelter. She'd been left there by the farmer who'd driven her in. He couldn't drive the car any further because the station had been bombed and the roads were gone and there were dead bodies and rail track and parts of the station scattered all over. So he left her there at the station and she came looking for our house which had been hard because there was nothing for her to get her bearings. Mother thought she could get back to the main station if I would just be quiet. I was trying to sing a lullaby for Rudi while I carried him on my back: Go to sleep, do not stir, for the angels are near. They will rock you in their arms, they will . . . She told me to shut up because the song was getting on her nerves. I knew she was too confused to know right from left. She said she'd seen people wandering about looking for the Red Cross who were making a collection place so people could be taken out of the city. She said it was near the station so I said, Yes, we'll go there, and I took over and led the way. But when we got closer to the Hauptbahnhof there were refugees and slave labourers like ants running from fire. A freight train full of refugees had come in from the east which had got caught in the bombing and bodies were sprawled on top of one another in the open carriages, piles of them, and they seemed to be stuck together. The platforms and the rooms and the central waiting area of the station were all collapsed, and there were children wandering among the corpses calling for their mothers. In the bricks and rubble there were bodies and parts of bodies and everything was still burning and the smell was like

133

pigs roasting. I pulled Mother away and we left the station and went to the square. Buses were lined up to take children to the children's home outside the city. We wouldn't let Rudi go with them. We kept him. Sometimes Mother carried him and sometimes I did. He didn't cry at all and his eyes were wide open looking at everything, but of course being fourteen months old he didn't understand what he was seeing. Once I thought he might be blind and waved my hand in front of his face but luckily he grabbed my hand so I knew he was okay.

Mother looked at me as we were sitting close together waiting to see if anyone would come and help us and she said, It's Ash Wednesday. She started laughing like a crazy person and I almost had to slap her but then suddenly she stopped. It was late now and colder and people were getting frantic. I said to Mother. Let's go. There's nothing here. Let's get to the Grosser Garten and perhaps Aunt Hilda's house will still be there. That cheered her up though I didn't think Aunt Hilda's house would still be there, but we started walking and others were going that direction too. Now you couldn't see the columns of black smoke hanging over Dresden because it was dark but the charred paper and debris was still falling from the sky and Mother was always wiping Rudi's face with her hand and our skin was black and there wasn't a star in the sky. The rain had stopped. The thuds kept on as chimney pots and walls kept falling down. We kept walking because I thought I could smell the River Elbe and I wanted the pleasure steamers and barges to still be sailing on the river and for the banks to still have vendors selling cake and coffee and we could lie down in the meadow gardens and sleep.

On the corner of Parkstrasse there was such a high pile of rubble you couldn't see over it and we had no strength to climb it or go round it to reach the park. But it made some shelter and Mother couldn't go on, so we huddled together there with some other people and it was a comfort to be with others, and if you didn't get too close to the burning rubble, warmth came off it and we were glad because it was freezing cold and everything was so wet from the rain but our faces were burning. Mother had a little suitcase with dry clothes for Rudi and she put them on him. There was a woman who was pregnant who was trying to get to a café in the park where they'd set up a maternity home. She told us people were moving out of Dresden like an army and that perhaps the bombing would start again. My hands started shaking very badly when she said that so I sat on them so Mother wouldn't see.

We were woken by the sound of the sirens and it was terrible because now hearing them was very different from before. We began screaming because there was nowhere to go. If there was a cellar it was full of people crouching in the dark and wet and they wouldn't let anyone in. There were very few shelters because no one had thought Dresden would be bombed. A relative of Winston Churchill's lived in Dresden and we thought they'd leave us out of it. We got up and began to run this way and that but we didn't know where to go and the sirens kept on and people were shutting up their ears and the children started screaming all over again. And we waited for the fire-bombs to whiz through the air and turn us into firewood. The pregnant woman stayed with us because she'd got attached to Rudi and she was on her own anyway and I didn't want her to be that way. She was pretty in spite of that sticking-out belly and she was kind, especially to Rudi. She gave him some of her water. She said to me, Let me hold him a little. And I knew what she was thinking. The other people who'd been with us went toward the park, but I didn't want to, it was so open, and also someone said the animals had been let out of the zoo which was burning and I'm afraid of tigers and crocodiles so I told Mother, No, we must go to the

Aldstadt. And Gisela, the pregnant woman, she agreed and so we started that way. And now we could hear a drone that became a loud roaring in the sky and the flares were lighting up everything and for a moment I was transfixed by them they were so pretty like Christmas lights falling through the darkness. Mother had to slap me to make me stop looking and move. We hung onto each other and we just ran and ran. The bombs started falling and there was no shelter because all the buildings were blown apart and if there was a basement it was barricaded by debris. Mother hung onto me and I to her, and the pregnant woman held my other hand and we ran on waiting to be hit by the bombers.

We were still alive until we turned the corner of a church and we ran into where a bomb had just fallen and we'd run into hell. Flames were fifty feet high, the air was on fire and so bright you couldn't look, it was like staring at the sun. An armchair sailed past a window and girls were flying with wings of fire. When the earth split open bodies fell down into the ravine and disappeared, their voices coming up for a minute like last goodbyes. Trees were uprooted and they blew down the street knocking people over. Everywhere were people all black and twisted, some in piles where they'd stampeded, and then there were people like the boy sitting against walls as if they'd fallen asleep and they looked all right but they were dead. Some people were running round in circles with all their clothes ripped off and their skin burning bright. Bodies were hanging from trees and up ahead where the office buildings were hit we could see people jumping out of windows, the women's skirts ballooning as they came down slowly while the men came down quick like bricks. We were screaming all of us screaming and some just standing still with their mouths open. I don't know who was holding Rudi, Mother or me, I don't know who it was who was holding him. We held fast to one another and were trying to get to the high railings round the church. It looked as though a giant had stepped on it, but around it were high railings set in concrete and everyone huddled behind them to stop being pulled into the flames. An old man was thrown against a wall and a dog was hurled through a window and others were being sucked into the burning fire, mothers and children spinning for a moment and then it was scarlet and for a moment it was beautiful because there were the blue and pink scarves of light coming out and it was quick to die. A mighty wind was coming up from the earth and sucking in air from all sides and pulling everything in, in, in. I saw people melt and skin drip like lard and I turned to look for the pregnant woman but she hadn't been able to keep up with us. I wanted to get her behind the church railings with us, and I got up but Mother screamed NO. And I saw Gisela running with her arms out ahead of her but then her belly split and the baby was hanging there from its cord with its little arms down.

And now when you come into the room Frieda it's different because now I am that mighty wind that sucks everything. I don't even look up I can't stop my hand is taking everything out of my brain and putting it down and I can't stop I'll go on to the end so maybe then I'll forget not remember And I see your face and you say stop now, it's enough and you grab and shake me And I say Oh great, now I can stop. Wonderful. Thanks a lot. I turn to her and now I'm really a wreck, more than Mother, screaming and crying and I say Frieda I can't remember I can't remember who was holding Rudi who was holding him because I can't remember. I'm sobbing till my face is all buckled like the railings we hid behind and I can't breathe any more And you keep saying, It's okay. It doesn't matter who was holding him. It doesn't matter. I'm howling like a wolf and all I want to do is to put my fingers into my eyes and poke them out but I can't because what would Mother do without me so all I can do is pick up the pen and write until the end and then I can maybe if I'm lucky die.

I remember this: after the bombing stopped and the mighty wind died we started to walk toward the hospitals because we'd heard they were still there.

I remember this: people in a trance and we with them sleep-walking on our legs. The wardens had turned into rescue teams and there were soldiers and they were telling people what to do because everyone had forgotten. The wardens had blankets and they put them round us and we waited for trucks to come to take the bombed-out people to Neustadt. We got onto a truck and were taken somewhere outside the city that wasn't burning. Going out on the truck I can't remember or only little falling pieces that go thud, thud, thud. How we got there and who was with us I can't remember, only it was the day after the second day of bombing, so that makes three days of bombing and each time twice they came in the planes at night and again in the day. They were trying to get every one of us. It was only when we got off the truck that I saw you, oh God, Frieda, I couldn't believe it was you and you saw me at the exact moment and we ran towards each other with our arms out and though your hands were covered in bandages and it hurt you to hold me you did.

We went back into Dresden again, and I don't know why, or even how I remember doing it because every day pieces keep dropping off and soon if you look through me there'll be nothing but air. The other stuff I wrote has disappeared or burnt up by which I mean I can't remember it any more. But I said to you, I must go back into the city and you said, I'll go with you. We were mad, we hadn't changed our clothes for a week, we wandered around in the house and in the garden but we didn't know what to do with all that green around us, all those things that weren't dead.

138

There were bunches of white lilac draped over the brick wall and I couldn't understand how they were still breathing and the pink tulips confused me by opening. I wanted to see if Aunt Hilda was still alive with my cousins. You never knew, sometimes a person who'd been stuck in a cellar had got out and were alive. You wanted to try to find your uncle because you'd been going to see him when the tram exploded and you were thrown on the burning road. Your uncle pulled your hands, one by one, finger by finger, out of the road that was bubbling and sticky like boiling toffee and your handprints were left behind in the road. That's what you told me and it was as if you were telling about someone else's hands. And I hate to think it because I have no pain that shows and I cannot imagine how you're still able to think or talk at all. I thought I was smarter than you and braver and now I'm the one in pieces not you.

They didn't bomb the hospitals because there were big red crosses on white backgrounds laid out on the roofs of the hospitals and even the English and the Americans could understand that much. But everything else was gone, so why we went back I'm not sure, but we had to. We were living in this house, but all day we didn't know what to do with ourselves. We had to go back to Dresden. We could leave Mother because now she was so quiet it was spooky. It was fifteen miles and we walked and on the road and up ahead others were walking. There was nothing to see in the distance but smoke and when it lifted there was just the sky without spires and turrets, without the clock tower, without the long lines of upright brick houses, without the delicate iron work of the balconies with the angels flying and the roses and spikes and the roofs like Hansel and Gretel and the windows like circles of light. There was no overhead railway and no lamps with their flame heads and no trams or cars or boys on bicycles and like a dreamer I was looking for the museum, and for my school and the

state bank on the corner, the high office buildings and the opera
house and the triumphant arches. I looked for the beautiful dome
of the Frauenkirche which I always lifted my eyes to see but it
wasn't there, nor were the stone saints and if there were statues
they had no heads on and if there were angels they had no wings.
You said, Did God get out of Dresden? And I said, Not a chance.
Burned like the rest.

We walked and it got harder as we came closer to the city where the
debris began to cover the road and where they'd piled up corpses
that looked like twisted rusted metal lying in puddles of rain. And
there was a box of naked dead babies. Military jeeps and relief
trucks kept blaring their horns and pushing us off the road, and
refugees were pulling carts and prams piled high with boxes of
their junk. The closer we got to the city, the more jammed the road
became and parts of the tramlines were twisted and sticking up in
the air because that's what happens to train and tram lines when
bombs hit them. Inside the city there were women like scavengers
in the open places, digging for wood and charcoal, digging for food
in cans because all the bakeries and food stores were gone. A boy
was digging with a knife to pull out pieces of wood from under the
tramlines. In one place someone had turned on a hydrant and
women were trying to wash clothes in buckets, bending over like
peasants, having on their heads scarves because they didn't have
hair. It was not so cold and if it wasn't for the smoke you might
think it was spring coming, or that things could come back from
the dead since there was a tuft of green blooming in a black tree
trunk and one purple flower in a garden of dead bushes, but if it
was spring how could it be? We had to keep cloth to our faces
because of the stench. A truck driver gave us a ride. He told us peo-
ple were being shipped out on the Elbe to Pirna and did we want
to go. You said no. We were looking for our families, you said. He
smiled in that way people smile when you say that. He drove into

what used to be the Aldmarkt and we looked and there was nothing but an old man sitting on the ground and people digging among the ruins like black crows on a skeleton. They'd made caves and were living in them, you could see them crouched in the empty space surrounded by broken walls, lighting fires like Stone Age people. The clocks were all stopped and the bells were silent. In one place I saw a house that was standing all by itself, perfect, surrounded by ruins, and a woman was hanging clothes on a clothes line and inside through the window you could see people eating at a table. I thought it was one of those things people see when they're mad. You agreed that we couldn't have seen it. A soldier said to us, The Altmarkt will soon be a crematorium. Leave the city. They were bringing the dead out of cellars, but most of those cellars were too hot to go into and the German soldiers were backing away and they were trying to make the slave labourers and prisoners do it but if our soldiers wouldn't they'd be shot just like the rest. The centre of the city was blocked off and flamethrowers were burning the dead on grids. Bodies and parts of them were being shovelled up into heaps with forks and spades to be burned. We watched for a while. They were going to take them out of the city to be buried in mass graves, but by the time the burning had finished there wasn't much left to be buried. Then the bulldozers came. We just looked because now we were used to it.

Everywhere we went there were people calling, calling, calling . . . and digging in the ruins around a house or cellar that once was home, and pinning messages or scraps of cloth to doors and walls – Come home. Don't come home. Find Hans. Write to this address in Munchen. Have you seen Lisa? Where are you, Daddy? Police were ordering people not to come back to try to find what they'd left behind, but they wouldn't listen. They kept looking, kept calling into houses. When we reached where we thought the bakery should be it wasn't there. I said, Frieda, I just need to find Aunt

Hilda's house and then we can leave. We started walking again. I was holding your arm instead of holding your hand the way we used to. We said not a word to one another, you and I, but we kept on walking and I looked because part of me was thinking I might see one of the boys or girls we knew, or even Aunt Hilda in her silly purple hat with that big leather bag that was always full of stuff to wipe a nose or shut up a bawling child. I hoped one of the boys might come around the corner and yell in our faces the way they used to. Sometimes in the dust I almost thought I saw people I knew, but if there were ghosts it was only the blue curtain blowing in the upstairs window or the hotplate where sausages and potato cakes once fried in butter. In the rubble there might be a broken bowl or a crushed painting or a chair on its side and you might see a step on which a girl had once sat to tie her shoes. It was then that I knew all the things were gone and that there was nothing to show that we'd lived there or had even lived at all. The only living things were rats, fat and bloated, with red eyes, waddling in and out of the rubble with their abdomens about to split, making a low grunting sound like pigs. One jumped out with a shriek because the rubble was burning him from underneath. And if there were flying things they were only the vultures from the zoo or swollen birds that sat flat on the ground because there were no poles or window sills to perch on, no ledges, no telephone wires, no trees or bushes and the sky so thick and dark and brown they couldn't use it. If there was a door half buried in rubble there'd be a note on it for the family who'd once lived there with an address to find so-and-so or a scribble in chalk on a wall saying someone was looking for their wife or mother and to please come: Ich suche meine frau. Wir leben. EB und JB. Mutti, wo bist du?

∽ 14 ∾

Kurt read all night. He could hear the ticking of his clock and the thud, thud, thud of his heart. He stared at the illuminated numbers on the clock but they didn't make sense. He felt dizzy and lay still. As he pulled the sheet up around him, his hand met the pile of papers and his fingers moved instinctively away. He tried to get up but his legs didn't work and when he dragged himself out of bed he fell to the floor. He sat with his back against the bedframe, his hands over his head. There was a soft weight against his chest. He drew his arms around it protectively and closed his eyes. Church beams were turning to kindling, the gold cross melted on the altar and pooled on the stone floor. The earth and sky were rocking and women came flying by like angels. The wind was playing a tune on a piano and a dog vanished into the trees with a baby in its mouth. Mouths were pressed up against railings, trying to gulp air. He was near the front and could feel himself being pushed forward as more bodies were thrown against the railings, the dead shoving as hard as the living. When the railings buckled and collapsed, bodies fell forward, each layer putting out the screams of the layer beneath. For a second there was a clear open space in front of him and in that second, like a rip in his body, something was torn away from him. It flew through the smoke and vanished into the furnace. The emptiness he felt was so intense he fainted.

Someone was banging furiously at the door, calling his

143

name. He stumbled up and went to the door and opened it. Mr Patel, the motel owner, was squinting at him. Are you all right? People are calling me, not able to get hold of you, what shall I be telling them? The sunlight made Kurt recoil, and he pulled back into the room. Mr Patel's round face was concerned and suspicious at the same time. What is going on here?

I haven't been well, Kurt said. But I'm okay now.

Mr Patel nodded. Otherwise my brother is a doctor.

Kurt put his hand up to his eyes, feeling dizzy for a moment, Thank you, he said. I'm okay.

You will call the office if anything is needed?

I will. Kurt moved back, closing the door. He sat down on the bed, his head tipping forward in a slow sustained movement until his head hit his knees. There was a humming in his brain as if he were trapped in a hive. He held onto the side of the mattress; his body was so light it might take to the air and fly. Desperately trying to get back to the present, he began walking back and forth, trying to connect his feet to the floor, himself to now. He walked unsteadily into the bathroom, holding onto the walls for support, and took a shower, letting the cold water run over him, standing under the torrent until his skin simmered down and cooled. Afterward he was less shaky and he could think more coherently. He called Hannah, but when he heard her voice he didn't have anything to say. He asked her what day it was. She said, Wednesday. He hesitated, I need a map, was all he could say.

What kind?

A German map.

She became alert and focused. Is there a library?

I think so.

Okay, she said calmly, find it and go get a map off the

net. Start there.

Right, he said.

I'm coming to Dresden, she said.

At the Dresden library he got a World War II map of Germany off the Net, along with aerial shots showing the ruins of all the blitzed cities, and a detailed one of Dresden, dated 18.4.45, two months after the fire-bombing. He took copies to the print store and had them blown up to poster size and once he got everything back to his room, he propped them up against the walls and studied them until he'd memorized the locations and names of the main cities and towns. He went to Frieda's house and she came back to his motel room; the two of them sat on the floor in front of the maps as slowly, carefully, Frieda began to piece his mother's history together, making red circles round the towns they'd passed through. She charted the retreat out of Dresden into the suburb and, although she couldn't remember the name of the place, she had perfect recall of what followed: the long, slow march south with hordes of other starving refugees. She pointed out the towns and villages they'd settled in for short periods, where she'd worked on farms, and where his mother had worked in a clinic. They'd kept moving, often leaving in the middle of the night when things became overcrowded or there was no food or when predators with guns chased them out of their makeshift shelters or barns. They would wander for weeks with no destination in mind, trying to keep off the main roads, sometimes catching a ride on the back of a truck, or hiding out in a bombed house waiting for the rain to stop. Early one morning they'd broken into a barricaded house to find a family of Jews hiding in an attic. They didn't know the war was over and didn't know what to do now that it was.

When a train roared by, Frieda said, we ran after it helplessly, waving our arms, screaming for it to stop. One time we came upon one of these trains, it had stopped where the line ran out and now refugees were setting up house in the carriages, putting up curtains, making fires between the carriages, finding a separate carriage for people who had cholera and marking it with a black cross. We scoured the farmland for food, carrying water back to the train in steel helmets, sharing what we found because there were not so many of us. We moved on when we ran out of food. Another time, when we were unable to go any further because of the snow, your mother saw a Russian soldier throw a small child down an empty well. She was about to throw herself in after it: she thought she could catch the child before it hit the bottom. She was so distraught she disappeared into the woods for days before I found her. Eventually we reached Gera, Frieda said, pointing it out, and we walked from there to Wurzburg and down into the refugee camp in the American sector.

Kurt charted his mother's journey on the poster board, marking the distances she'd walked, and how many miles between each of the places she'd passed through. He was trying also to make some kind of time-line from the day of the flight from Dresden to the day she and Frieda, with their mothers, had flown from the American Army base to Paris and from there by boat to New York. It took him all day, going back and forth to the library and print shop, until he'd pieced together a detailed map of Dresden, and another map of his mother's wandering life after Dresden. He'd done it in a frenzy, not stopping to eat or drink till it was done. And there it was, at long last, his mother's story,

146

with pictures, laid out neatly on the floor of a motel. On an impulse, he took out his E-ticket to Memphis, and saw that he'd left New York on February 13th, the day he and Hannah had met; the first day of the fire-bombings of Dresden in 1945.

After he'd taken Frieda back home, he lay on the bed and more details came back: the small moon-shaped scars on his mother's face, and how, when she was angry they'd flare up and when she was depressed they were like ivory discs on her cheeks. She was back now, and he could remember sewing with her, around five, before his father came home. He returned to the room where the two of them sat sewing together: his mother was talking in a disjointed way about her childhood, about the flight from Dresden and he was trying to keep up with her, making small stitches as she spoke, trying to hold it all together. When he fell asleep he dreamed of bomber planes flying in perfect formation through a clear blue sky, they were so beautiful that he woke up weeping. He let himself weep, shutting out the martial voice in his brain that kept ordering him to be a man. He fell asleep again and again in quick intense blasts and when he woke he thought that by now Hannah would be driving to Dresden; she'd come the way he had, following his tracks. It was a comfort to him. He remembered her physical beauty, her strength, her laugh, her capacity for affection and sweetness, and he was reminded of the love he felt for her and the solid security of her body, and of his own, when they made love. He imagined her driving through the swamplands, gazing out at the landscape bleached by the spring sunshine as a cold wind moved through trees still only half in leaf, fragile enough to be wiped out by a single frost.

His mind was all over the place, as if trying to locate itself back in the present. Soon he was wondering why the Civil War had marked the South in the particular way it had, so that Mississippi lay in the dust like the skeleton of a dog, Alabama shimmered with some kind of forsaken beauty, and Louisiana was drowned in sorrow. Everywhere was darkened by Faulkner's sense of the dead – the faded forgotten ruts, the ghost of an occasional passage, the end of life as it had been, before the war, before it happened. And, at that moment, he was filled with deep sorrow for Dresden – for all the Dresdens of the world. In his grief he could hear Germany's silence at his back like a freezing wind, holding off memory and horror, shutting off mourning and redemption. And it struck him for the first time how difficult it was, how impossible, to be German. For who could stand up and say I'm proud to be German? Could the new pope pull that off, or would it start European knees shaking all over again? And the old pope, the Polish ground-kisser: no one found him excessive or nationalistic, but imagine for a minute the German pope on his knees with his lips pressed to German soil.

15

Hannah didn't come to his motel; instead, she found her way to Frieda's doorstep, having got the address in the phone book at the post office on the square. A cashier had been happy to point her in the right direction: Keep straight on to the end of the road, right-hand side, black door, No. 22. Can't miss it. She pulled up on the left-hand side and looked across at a house with a neat fence, a door with dead honeysuckle clutching at the white wall, struggling to come back to life. And there was the step where Kurt must have slept the night when he'd first come to Dresden. Blossom was coming out on the trees and the leaves were uncurling. Where the road ended and the woods began she saw a dead tree, and out of the split trunk a riot of new life bubbled up like green froth on the water when frogs are mating. The mourning doves were calling out their notes, time and again, like a lament. She got out of the car and crossed the road. Frieda opened the door, wiping her hands on an apron. Fraulein Hannah, she said, please come in. Kurt told me about you.

Hannah looked around her, scanning the room up ahead of the hallway, looking quickly sideways into a living room hidden in semi-darkness, her face glowing with expectation.

He's not here, Frieda said.

Oh. Hannah's face fell. I thought he'd be here. I was sure he'd be here.

Well, Frieda said, he will be coming later. He was taking

some books back to the library. Come, I'll make you some-thing to eat. It's lunchtime, ja? No, don't protest, you look like you might also sometimes forget to eat.

I hope I'm not intruding?

How could you be? As soon as Hannah was safely installed in the chair with the red cushion, Frieda asked, Now, tell me, where did your people come from in Germany?

Hamburg.

That went before us, she said, in '43. And with that something collapsed and opened up at the same time and the two of them began to speak German, hesitantly at first and then picking up speed, filling the bright spick and span American kitchen with the guttural, throaty sounds and laughter of the cruel language.

So how's it been to have Kurt back? Hannah said, look-ing around her at some blue-and-white china on a shelf and noticing how comfortable she felt with Frieda, seeing in her gestures something of her own grandmother, some-thing particularly European: a more sombre view of life, steeped, distilled and fragile, wrought out of history and tragedy into a different sensibility, one as timeless and indestructible as granite.

You know, Frieda said, when he came, Kurt, it was the exact same time as with his mother. It's wonderful to have him here again, but for me it's strange and sometimes sad. I see him like someone fallen into a dream that's over long ago, but he keeps going, one foot ahead of the other, like a soldier. With a sudden jerk, she said, Can you imagine what it must have been like for the soldiers to come back after the war? Waiting all that time for the horror to end so they could come home only to find that where before there'd been cities and houses now there was nothing?

You think it's like that for Kurt?

Maybe I do, a bit, he is wandering around in ruins, picking up pieces of rubble now and then, trying to find what has been lost for sixty years.

Should he have left it buried?

Frieda smiled. Once, I'd have said yes. But he had no choice; the past came to him and he had to follow it.

I know you talked a lot, Hannah said, and I wondered if there were things you chose *not* to tell him?

Frieda tipped her head to one side with interest. How straight you are, the way you ask this. You want to know those things – to keep them for when he can hear them?

Hannah hesitated. I thought you might know something more about his mother's death.

He was so upset by it that I didn't want to say anything more and, besides, he didn't ask.

I think, Hannah said, he's been hoping desperately she'd still be alive. He must feel very lonely and vulnerable now.

Frieda got up, and headed for the sink where her silence was filled with the rush of water from the faucet, the business of filling the kettle, taking down small plates from the shelves and placing cake forks with china handles on a blue-tiled tray. When she'd put them close to Hannah she leaned forward with her hands flat on the table and looked directly at her: You are a doctor?

I have a PhD in psychology. Why do you ask?

Frieda sat down and pushed her hair back with her hands and nodded. You were right, she said. There are things about his mother that I haven't told him. She frowned, reached over and touched Hannah's arm. I think also it's not my business to say something like that to him; he needs to know it when he is able to remember for himself. So

151

– Frieda looked across – I can only tell what I know, and you must decide what to do. I told him that Else disappeared after Wilhelm died, and that I tried to find her but couldn't. I thought she was trying to lose me because I was the last person from the old world, and maybe she didn't want to remember any of it. But after I'd given up all hope of finding her, and I kept looking for several years, I was contacted by a hospital. She'd had a breakdown and had been institutionalized. She was asking for me and I went to see her . . .

Wait, wait, Hannah said, leaning forward and nearly tipping over the cup. How exactly did that happen?

Frieda smiled. Kurt asked them to telephone me.

He knew?

At that time he did. Now, I'm certain he has forgotten about that time. But, then, after they called, he asked me to come see her with him. Understand, I hadn't seen him for years because he stopped coming here once he was grown, at school, at college, after that he didn't come. So it was an emotional meeting for us. By then he'd been seeing her for some time. He went once, twice a week to visit her. He was very loving, very patient, with her. He'd made sure she had a room of her own and he'd brought some things of hers there, pictures – one of Dresden with the river – and a table and chair, and, Frieda smiled, even her sewing machine. The room was very neat, and she took care of the way she looked, but she had only one expression: a stare that was empty. Kurt would talk to her slowly, and sometimes she'd reply and sometimes she'd just shrug. Frieda's voice became fierce and protective. Understand, please, Else was remote, even a bit cold with him, but she wasn't a crazy person. We walked in the garden with her, she held his hand, she responded to things. She was extinguished, that's all. It was the word Kurt used about her, without knowing why it was the right word. Frieda got up, walked to the French doors, stood there a moment, and then walked back again. You see, at the hospital, she didn't remember me. I'm not even sure she remembered Kurt. Not really. Once I asked her some stupid thing – there was a lilac tree in the grounds of the institution and I asked her if she remembered the one in her childhood home. We used to make houses under it and played there with our dolls. I was just making talk but she looked at me with a wide-open look, alert and clear, and she smiled. It was behind the linden trees, she said. Frieda shook her head. For me, this was very upsetting. That she could go back and find that tree when everything else was gone. It distressed me for days. I did not go to see her again. Sometimes Kurt sent me a note and sometimes I wrote to her but she didn't reply. And then he told me she had died. I went, of course, for the funeral. We buried her, the two of us. She opened her hands in misery. Now I see, telling you, that I should have told him this also.

Hannah took Frieda's hand and held it, turning it slowly so she could see the empty palm, the life-lines burned away and, lifting Frieda's hand, she rested it for a moment on her cheek and kissed it. Frieda's dark eyes were locked on Hannah's, tears brimming, about to fall. Do you know where the hospital was? Hannah asked.

In the Bronx. I wish I could remember exactly where . . .

It's okay. I can find it if he wants to go back.

After a pause, Frieda said, You care so much about him, and you want so much to help him, but I wonder about it. Frieda smiled, I think you are in love with him.

Hannah looked up, startled, and gave a soft laugh.

All the time, though, Frieda said, you are using your

head, trying to understand him that way. Or is it just that we Germans are not permitted to feel with our hearts? Or we do not permit it for ourselves? When I saw those pictures of the bodies in the concentration camps and the yellow faces with the eyes in black sockets and bones coming through skin, I understood that we were responsible because we were there – that is enough. Her head dropped and the anger was gone. I have never spoken of these things. To whom could I say them? I used to think, before Kurt came here this time, that we stayed silent out of fear, but now I think also that we stayed silent so as not to see ourselves as victims. This would make us despise ourselves even more. And so last year when they made the memorial to the Jewish dead in Berlin, with those burial stones right on top of where the Reichstag and the Wilhelmstrasse used to be, when I saw that, something came tumbling down inside me. For the first time I felt a little peace. Under the memorial lies the debris of the Third Reich . . . I read about it in the paper, I saw it on the television . . . I heard the American architect say he made it so that when you walk there you see what lies beneath, the buried gardens, the bunkers, the bones of Nazis, all that underground life that ended in death. So now in Berlin people are walking on the dead. When Herr Schroeder opened it he looked himself like a ghost, and I felt pity for him. He was shaking when he stood up and said: 'Today we open a memorial that recalls Nazi Germany's worst, most terrible crime – the attempt to exterminate an entire people.' When he said those words, Frieda said, something stopped burning.

She looked up. And now boys skateboard and smoke there, girls sit on the stones and laugh and tie their shoes, and mothers stop to feed their babies, and already the graffiti has come and people write what they like, even anti-Semitic, and now we see it all because it is on top of the ground . . . The Holocaust is out on the streets and they are walking by it on the way to work, and perhaps now we can speak of our own sorrows also.

The door opened and they both turned, startled, to hear Kurt's voice, calling for Frieda. He strolled into Frieda's kitchen and, when he saw the two women together, his face beamed. With his arrival, the sombre atmosphere of the room shattered. Hannah stared at him. He looked different. He stood up straight as if a weight had fallen off his back. He walked quickly over, pulled them up from their chairs and took them, one in each arm, and drew them together. He turned to Hannah and said, You didn't tell me you were here. She shrugged. Now and then, she said, I get this irresistible urge to flee the city – just couldn't stop myself.

∽ NEW YORK ∽

16

Kurt's birthday cake, made from a recipe in Hannah's egg-splattered *Joy of Cooking*, sat on a glass stand strewn with rose petals. On the floor surrounding the table, thirty-three votive candles floated on discs of water, and everywhere he looked were spectacular arrangements – lilac and lilies, white peonies with scarlet centres, sprays of pink-tipped rhododendrons. It was the first time he'd been to her New York apartment and he was moved by it, by the presence of a life he knew nothing about, being taken into it, and on his birthday, too. They sat close together and his hand covered hers, brown against white. He whispered something into her throat and she pulled him to her while her other hand slid down the side of his body in a way that was both intimate and comforting.

I bought this place for the floor, she said, turning her head toward a stunning emptiness, pumpkin-pine hardwood, glossy as gold, high walls ending in a blue ceiling. When I've had a really stinking day I come home and dance. Ballet. I was pretty good, but I couldn't really pursue it at the time. What about you?

Didn't take up dancing.

You went to one of those school where they fence and row, didn't you?

I did. But I was never much of a team player. Running. Long distance, that's what I loved. And yes, fencing, did a bit of that too.

It shows, she said.

Is that a dig?

Not at all.

Anyway, he said, passing her the cake knife, how d'you know it was my birthday?

The way we know everything about you: driver's licence. Say you'd lost it? Or you didn't have your ATM card? What then?

He gave her an ironic smile. I've been blessed, no doubt about it. Thing is, you noticed the date on my licence and remembered it . . . Other birthdays came back to him in small precise detail: his mother making him a cake in the shape of a Gothic church, beautiful, ornate, and how he'd loved the fact that the number 10 was written in gold on the face of the clock tower. His thirtieth birthday, in London, at a club, Ronnie Scott's. And he was right there, squashed in a corner listening to jazz with a woman, who suddenly laughed. Her teeth, perfect and pearly. The sound of her laughter, pungent and sexy, her wrist-watch, tiny, gold. She was gone as quickly as she came.

I always remember people's birthdays, Hannah said. It's a selfish kind of thing: had some spectacularly empty birthdays so I've been making up for it ever since.

And the beauty? The largesse? All this? His hand drew in the cool sophistication of the space. Her eyes followed his glance and came back to him; she bit her lip, and her face was so glowing that he was forced to kiss her. She smiled. Just a reaction to a time of poverty. She looked at him, How about eating your cake? She ate hers with her fingers. The largesse, she repeated thoughtfully. Well, we may've been reduced to white trash, she said, taking a sip of champagne, but I come from an elegant crowd on my mom's side. Good German pedigree, pots of money from the gem trade, which was always referred to in our house

160

as the luxury-goods industry. We had salons in the Place Vendôme and Bond Street, but then of course there was the crash of the war and the flight out of Hamburg and it was all gone. After the war, my mom's family made a lot of their money back and plugged up the holes and losses. Marrying my dad was a dip, but it was manageable, until his company crashed. It was another catastrophe for my mother: she didn't think he could recoup his losses, or himself, and she was right. Everything went, including all her personal jewellery, a lot of it old and fabulously valuable. That's when Tallulah came in.

He reached across to rescue a bright shaving of hair which had got caught in her earring, and asked, Has she ever seen this place?

No. Her voice dropped. One day maybe she will. I'm less angry with her now. After what you found, back there, it's made me think about my grandmother and what she went through, and how that's affected my mother: they were at each other's throats all the time. They were so connected in the disconnect and the rage. When you told me you needed a map, I looked up Hamburg on the net, and I got some info about the way it was in the 30s and early 40s when my grandmother lived there. I suddenly remembered she stayed there when the rest of them got out. I never understood how she was left behind like that – but it sort of explains her fury and the way her language was shot with words that seemed out of time and place: she'd call us refugees, or displaced persons and, in the middle of a conversation she'd hurl in words like exile, inferno, Diaspora and a whole host of Yiddish words we didn't understand. We thought she was a bit nuts, but it was the way she experienced the world.

And my mother – her voice slowed – there was a time

161

when she was full of life, and sharp as a whip. She had Valentino ball-gowns and beautiful shoes and changed outfits a couple of times a day. She read, even in the bath, even when talking on the phone, she was always reading something, and I got that from her. She'd talk about the houses of her childhood and it was so thrilling to me – grand homes on Long Island Sound, money coming from centuries of intellectual elitism and commercial savvy. There was such beauty, the way she described it, it was like Scarlett O'Hara's mansion, surrounded by a jetty hung with boats, an acre of Italian garden, sumptuous parties with cars from New York parked ten deep around the stables, and a full orchestra on the lawn. My grandmother was a classical violinist before the war. Things were whispered about that, but I never heard her play. Hannah pressed her forefinger into the crumbs of cake and put them in her mouth. I don't think I told you this, she said cautiously, but my dad was ripped off by his partner, who was a cousin of my mother's, got very sordid, went to court. Actually, you're right: he did end up in jail. He was a high-class burglar. Very cool and smooth, not a scruple in the house. Real sonofabitch. No one recovered from that. My parent's marriage crashed on it. My dad's insurance business had been floated by my mother's side, and when Max cleaned the lot out and vanished, my father realized being CEO meant zilch if you have a crooked CFO who has wheezled himself into a position of absolute power and looted the place without you noticing it. Well, you're right, that's one way of looking at it: perhaps you do have to be a real sonofabitch to reach the corporate pinnacle, but isn't that because there's only room for one up there? She laughed, I know where you're going with that one, but perhaps another night, when it's not your birthday, we can talk about the sociopathology of corporate life.

As she got up to douse the candles on the cake, which were leaking wax onto the flowers, he looked at her taut, impatient body and saw within it a mind capable of enormous leverage; it was as compelling and urgent to him as his desire; it seemed to promise an end to his intellectual loneliness. He thought of being married to her and having that kind of companionship for the rest of his life. And out of nowhere, his business apprenticeship came up. He tried to shove it aside but it wouldn't budge: an MBA from Harvard, doing time as a rookie for a firm of brokers, a couple of heady years of spree-spending in the financial markets. He was looking down from a window on Wall Street, waiting for someone to sign a deal. The film reversed and he was loping backwards out of the room, through the door and out into the air where he felt the immensity of the skyscrapers and his own insignificance, followed by a sense that the deal was crooked and he'd go down with it.

A pungent smell of pickled red cabbage hung in the air. Tell me about the cooking, he said. Are we to be Germans together here?

You didn't like the spargelfest salad? I thought you liked beets.

I love beets and it was great – but I couldn't help but notice the stack of new German cookbooks in the kitchen and the printouts from germanfoods.org.

It's not an invasion.

Did I sound nervous?

You did.

I'm messing with you.

I've just finished reading Isherwood in German, she

said. Want to read it? It's really good. Not too many hard words.

I might need your help. He kissed her neck and drew his hand through her tangled hair. I really like it here, he said. There was something thrilling about being in a place she'd lived in, danced, dreamed and cooked in before she even knew he existed. He asked her, How d'you want it to be?

She stopped. With us? Can't we just find out?

I wonder where I'd be without you.

Oh, probably in Biloxi. You know, she said, sometimes I wonder how much relationship experience you've had. It's sort of weird not to know.

He laughed. Maybe we'll never know.

And sometimes, she said, there are days when I think this could work and other days when I think I must like train-wrecks. And I get impatient, wishing you'd find out more.

That bad?

Sometimes, she said, but maybe it's also the uncertainty of new love, not knowing from one minute to the next what the other person's feeling – it's so untried, unexpected. She leaned across as if she was going to tell him something secret but instead kissed him on the mouth, startling him, making him laugh. He held her by the back of her head and stared quietly into her eyes. I love you, Hannah Braun, he said.

He glanced sideways at the hallway that led into a wide open space full of rosy light that whooshed up to the ceiling, catching on Victorian cornices; plump plaster cherubs, a narrow chandelier scattering circles of light. A wall of bright windows, outlined in blue, was ushering in twilight and a breeze blew which seemed to carry the smell of the sea. Hannah said it came from the fish restaurant on the corner. Light from tall lamps moved across the floorboards and got snuffed out at the back of the apartment where shade created a secret place: a scarlet wall that hid the private rooms from the scrutiny of the empty space. Earlier, when she'd helped him settle in, she'd shown him how a bookcase slid invisibly into a wall to reveal a closet behind it. And, as she made a space for his clothes by chucking hers on the floor, she said, My grandmother spent eight months in Hamburg hiding in a closet behind a bookcase waiting for papers or death, whichever came first.

Hannah was checking her email – only one, she said, I promise – just need to see if Miriam closed her deal. Using two fingers, she was speed-typing on a drawing board she used as a table while he loaded the dishwasher and tidied up the kitchen in a competent manner, trying to put things back in the right place. She left her laptop and walked over to the windows that looked down on Prince Street. It was awash with people: men in wife-beater tee-shirts and women in tiny floating dresses and backless tops. It looked like they'd grabbed the first piece of clothing they could lay hands on and rushed out of hibernation. He came and stood beside her and she said, What'll you do here? She was sliding the windows open and he helped her.

You mean while you're at work? He was looking across at a narrow cream building on the opposite side of the street, similar to the one they were in, with fire escapes and balconies, and for a split second the building was blown sky-high.

Yes, while I'm working – what'll you do?

He thought she sounded nervous. Probably thinking he was going to cut out at two in the morning again and, in that moment, he resolved not to put her through that, whatever it took from him. He moved his arm and slid his hand upward until it reached her breast and stayed there. He was looking into the windows at the top of the building across the way where a blue television screen flickered and a white lamp came on to reveal a table with a wine bottle on it. An American flag was draped like a dirty tablecloth over the spoke of a balcony. Far below, the trees were tinged with the early red of the season.

Will it bother you if I say I don't know?

Not if it doesn't bother you.

He turned her body round so she could see that the empty table was no longer surrounded by its circle of flickering candles. Now the diamond points of light led straight to the crimson wall with its narrow interior door that was the entrance to her secret domain. They followed the lights like sleepwalkers, whispering to one another, grateful that the next day was Saturday and would be followed by Sunday. Neither of them had really bothered to unpack. When he came back from the shower she was sitting in a dimpled cream chair next to a round table. He thought she was reading: he had a view of her arm and one side of her face, her face was tipped toward her shoulder and she seemed to be smiling and, for a split second, he saw a baby at her breast. A sense of her fertility washed over him and he was deeply aroused by it, feeling an ache, a broodiness, wanting to bury himself in her. When they lay together and he entered her, her body kept opening until it became quick and alive, a hive buzzing and rocking with feverish wings, putting out honey that flooded the combs. All the layers of her body, above and below him, side by side and upside down of him were vibrating with heat. Her breasts were heavy and her body moved with his until there was nothing between them but sweat: he rubbed it from her cheeks and eyes, his lips skimmed the arch of her neck and he held her with his eyes and felt the pure joy of giving himself away. Their skin dried under the waves of the overhead fan, and they began a soft, fumbling conversation in a tongue not their own, in a language no longer cruel: Have you ever been so happy in your life?

17

Most mornings found Kurt seated at a table in Balthazar's on Spring Street. With Hannah at work, he was often adrift; his moods slipped and images from his mother's past haunted him. He woke covered in sweat and sometimes couldn't locate himself in time or wondered why he was where he was – on a street he didn't know, in parts of the city he had no reason to visit. His habits had changed, too. Where once he'd read the *Wall Street Journal* every morning, he now read the *New York Times*, avoiding the business section. He was making his way through *Goodbye to Berlin,* finding German harder to read than to speak. He and Hannah were talking to one another in German now, mostly when they were in bed. They'd taken on the marathon of *The Magic Mountain* in the language it was written in: Hannah would read, aloud, five pages a night, astonished by her perseverance, since she'd sworn on first reading that she'd never go through that again. Now, nightly, they climbed the rocks and mountains, endured the endless meals and waited for the spots on the lungs to darken and the blood to be spat into the handkerchief as the sanatorium rooms emptied and filled and the pages rolled endlessly on.

Kurt was more patient than Hannah. He'd spend a good hour in the restaurant, drinking his coffee, watching the cluster of anxious smokers puffing outside the door like pariahs, calming himself by staring at the slow circular swish of the dark fans in the mottled yellow ceiling. He'd try without success to read the labels on the long lines of dusty wine bottles on their high perches and watched the bar-tender with his polishing rag swiping away the dark splashes of life. In the evening it was different, a whole new crowd would pack the bar. Before six was best and, if Hannah was travelling or going to be late, he'd come in for a glass of beer, half a lobster and a plate of cheese served with soft bread with hard, chewy crusts that tasted vaguely sour. Now and then he'd take a lobster home for Hannah. He liked to listen in on other people's conversation and had a knack of knowing exactly when a tense conversation would explode into a full marital dispute. He saw a woman running down a street, fast and furious, being followed by a man. There was something sinister about the scene. It took him to another street, a brownstone with a balcony, on which a woman stood, looking down, calling to him, and when he looked again, she'd gone.

He was trying to feel at home in the neighbourhood and for a while didn't leave it much. Reaching the perimeters was like coming to an electric fence. After a while, he became curious about his old life and used Hannah's laptop to get into his bank accounts. He remembered all the numbers. He had a lot of money. And no interest in it. He could get into his email, but didn't want to, nor did he want to know what was going on in a world that had once been so compelling. His addiction was broken and in the emptiness he was experiencing some of the agitation and shakiness of a recovering alcoholic; by the second week he was becoming antsy and impatient, vaguely annoyed that Hannah could work in a way he'd never been able to: how could she control the time she spent at work? How could she keep herself separate from the frenzy of now, now, now?

On a blustery mid-morning in March he was sitting at the bar of the brasserie, idly listening to two traders talking about an insider trading scam. He was reading *The Times* when a section of the print began to slip and blur. He couldn't make out all the words, but phrases stood out . . . alleged misrepresentations . . . private transaction . . . doubts about the integrity . . . defendant's counsel's view . . . SEC . . . substantial litigation risks . . . the company faces . . . the possibility of fraud . . . The words and their implications disturbed him. They seemed personal. He left in a hurry. That's when he started to walk in the old manner, for hours and hours, one foot in front of the other, barely stopping. When it began to get dark it was only Hannah who returned him to the neighbourhood. Once home he felt safe and had no idea what had set him off, something in a newspaper or some words that a couple of traders had said; the details became scrambled and slipped off the page.

The next day he set out with no destination or purpose. After a couple of hours of circuitous walking he ended up on Madison and 42nd Street and kept walking up. He was feeling fine, everything looked much as it always had and he stopped to buy Hannah a new handbag from Bebe and considered lunching at Smith and Wollensky, but decided against it. When he reached St Bart's Cathedral, it occurred to him that he was very tired and he walked in and sat in a pew close to the altar, looking up and around him. The ceiling had black lace ironwork lamps with sharp tips of light. He felt his eyes close involuntarily now and then and once fell asleep for a few minutes before jerking awake again. A dull pain began to pound at the edges of his temples. The curved high altar rocked for a moment and the yellow-and-gold marble glowed against the dark wooden latticework; the gold cross with its radiant spikes cast a shadow on the pale cross behind it and the Byzantine beauty of it made him weak with awe that was somehow inlaid with terror.

He got up to leave, but found that he was unable to get beyond the angel in the Baptistery Chapel who had caught him and was whispering, *Be not afraid*. She knelt with one raised knee, her head lowly and sad, her arms holding a shallow marble bowl of holy water. The curls in her hair rippled and there was something about the gash which parted her hair that caught and held his attention, but only for a second before it was snatched away to a wall plaque, which read: *To the glory of God and in loving memory of Elizabeth Worthington Delatour*. The name, *Elizabeth*, pounced at him, and there was something about the two small chairs in front of the altar that was heartrending, and something about the tragic and accepting face of Jesus that tore at him. Turning to leave, he smashed his arm on the wing of the angel and had to stop himself from running. He flung himself at the door to the street.

Outside, caught in the bright sunlight speeding up and down Park Avenue, he beheld the magnificence of the Mutual of America Building, the high temple with its cleansed and glittering glass, its power and glory. The girth and height of it demanded reverence as it stared down the dreams of millions of tiny humans dashing about at its base. And here, waiting to cross the street, he realized someone was staring at him, someone familiar who found him familiar too, and before he could get going a man in a suit and tie came leaping up to him with the enthusiasm of a stag. Kurt? How are you, buddy? Long time no see.

The man's name had gone entirely but the teeth with their gap in the middle were memorable, and Kurt managed to pull off a smile.

Heard you left Morgan Stanley? That place just keeps on haemorrhaging. Where'd you go, anyway? The man was staring at him, looking for a weakness, a break in the fur, a place to sink a fang. Citigroup, wasn't it?

I'm taking a break.

Great, but you were there for a bit, right? Kurt was sweating. The guy thought he'd been fired. Had he been fired? Kurt rallied and asked, You?

Things are going great. Hooked up with a small boutique, sick of the financial supermarkets, like a dog-pile in there. Even the classy shops have gotten desperate after that last crash. Hey, remember Al Wasserman? I joined up with him, securities division, safest place to be these days. Hey, look, I'm sorry, got to run. Catch up with you later. He flew off down the street toward the Helmsley Building, with the granite and glass mountain of Metlife dwarfing and highlighting its delicate Romanesque beauty. He stopped, turned and yelled back, Hey Kurt! Don't forget to say hello to Elizabeth for me, will ya?

So it was Elizabeth: the woman with dark hair, the one who'd dived off the bridge, laughed in the club, been pregnant. The images lined up like soldiers, one after the other. And now he was standing behind Elizabeth and she was looking at herself in the mirror while he placed a necklace of seed-pearls and rubies round her neck and closed the clasp. She smiled at him in the mirror and his

172

hands rested on her shoulders for a moment. He froze the frame and forced himself to fix on her face before it vanished. If she were in a police line-up he'd say he'd never seen her in his life, and yet she was gathering momentum, the images beginning to stick. He couldn't tell Hannah. Not yet.

A day later, he went back to the same neighbourhood, walking with purpose up East 36th. He found the building he was looking for, but he was early for his appointment so he found a coffee shop and ordered a latte. The man's voice and the name, Elizabeth, kept echoing in his mind. He'd been as spiky as a scorpion with Hannah the night before, trying to keep her at bay. In his hand was the Elizabeth bomb and, if he let her in, got close, she'd pull the pin. She knew something was wrong, and he'd fobbed her off, saying he was frustrated by what was going on, not knowing anything. She'd got impatient and couldn't understand why he wouldn't do something about it. She was right. He'd agreed to see the shrink she'd suggested back in Dresden and had made an appointment. Now he had to keep it. Only six minutes to go. He was terrified. He left the coffee shop and walked back, entering a discreet grey office building, barricaded with scaffolding. He kept checking his watch, looking up at the sky, seeing the outline of a plane, and then back at the door. He found the brass shingle he was looking for: Dr E. J. Sugarman. No doubt about it: desperation had brought him to this. And there was no way back.

He pushed the bell and was immediately buzzed in. Entering a small reception area with magazines and a water cooler, he was relieved to find it empty. He sat in the chair closest to the door and as far as possible from the small corridor he imagined led to Dr Sugarman's consulting room. Anticipating interrogations, he began his own: Who the hell was Elizabeth? Was she his wife? How could she be? There was no way she could be, but there was something about that yell on the street that strongly suggested wife, while he was to his best knowledge un-wived. So why would he believe a scumbag like that anyway? But why would the scumbag lie? Of course he could be divorced: he'd backtracked some time ago with Hannah on his original divorce story, which he'd thrown in at the time as a decoy in the days when questions threw him wildly off course. There was only one divorce between them, which was hers. So who was Elizabeth? Surely a man did not forget his wife? From that moment under the roof of the Mutual of America Building his composure had been blown. No question about that. But how could he bring this up to Hannah now? And on the flimsy say-so of a trader on Park Avenue whose name he couldn't even remember? Perhaps he was being confused with another Kurt? But then, to toss out his petty evasions, the man's name came rushing to the forefront of his brain: Ken Wilson, that's who it was. He banged the flat of his hand into his forehead: six months on a deal some years back when the guy had just moved over from bonds. That's all he got, but it was enough to establish legitimacy.

One more time he took himself through the familiar ruminations that kept him on the edge of insanity. The relationship with Hannah was moving towards a close and compatible commitment. It would be the worst possible time to bring up something like this. They'd reached emotional equilibrium. They were happy. He felt married to her. He wanted to be married to her. He was *going* to marry her. Maybe he could just wait a bit and tell her when he knew the answer. Found out some facts. She liked facts. And what was the point of bringing it up if he didn't know whether it was true or not? Not to mention her own dismal history with married men. He couldn't do that to her. All that uncertainty: it would smack of the Atlanta disaster all over again. And on top of it all, she'd too much on her mind right now after that messy mistrial and the board looking for blood and wanting round the clock assistance from her. Besides, if Elizabeth was his wife, he'd forgotten her, which must mean he couldn't possibly love her. For an hour, he actually started to play with the notion of constructing a brand new life for himself, with a new identity, but the spectre of bigamy came rushing in. It was followed by the boomerang that he might actually be wanted by the Securities and Exchange Commission. Had this set him off in the first place?

On the other hand, it was devastatingly simple: Tell the truth. Trust her.

A small, round man appeared from the hollow of the corridor wearing blue eyes in a face of indeterminate European origin, chiselled by time and history. He walked up and introduced himself with a gravity that seemed in keeping with Kurt's predicament. The minute Kurt was seated opposite him in the grey-walled, photoless room, he lost his capacity to speak. Dr Sugarman didn't help him out. Nor did he mention any connection to Hannah. Nor had Hannah told Kurt anything more about Dr Sugarman, just stayed in her neatly defined barriers and handed him a telephone number. She'd done it last night, after he'd gone silent on her. Perhaps it's time to do this now? She'd said it kindly enough but he'd been given his marching orders. He was on his own. No doubt about it. He felt his right foot begin to twitch repetitively and stopped it. Dr Sugarman had noticed it all right, and without looking down. They sat in silence for some minutes while Kurt stared at the doctor's shoes; filled as they were with utterly quiet feet, he found them annoying. The shoes were expensive and this made him wonder how much money could be made at this game. The doctor's hands were folded and his eyes roamed Kurt's face without staring. He sat in his chair with stately authority, not a flip of emotion on his face. Finally Kurt blurted out, I'm not sure where to start. At which Dr Sugarman actually spoke, his voice calm and without accent, Please tell me whatever's on your mind.

Kurt's nervousness, which had about it a strong taint of aggression, suddenly flew out of the window and the air cleared. Well, he said, I find myself with a serious problem that comes from an even more serious problem. It's possible I might have lost my mind. I've been trying to put the pieces of my mother's life together and during the process . . . Well . . . Let me back up a bit. I'm presuming you know nothing about me? Or do you? Did . . .? Well, I should say first that I've had some pretty bad amnesia . . . Do you know any of this? Has . . .?

Assume, Dr Sugarman said, that I know nothing.

Well, about two months ago I walked out of my house and I've never been back. I walked to my office, I couldn't go in and I've not been back there either. Since then I've been on the run, wandering and walking and driving for hundreds of miles. I went south out of some unknown compulsion. I met a woman and fell completely in love with her. Had I not met her I'd be in Alaska by now.

Anyhow, all my wandering took me to Tennessee and to a part of it I'd been before as a kid, only I didn't remember that, I just sort of ended up there, walking into a two-bit town called Dresden where I crashed on the doorstep of a woman who used to know me and my mother, had in fact left Germany with my mother after the war . . . and she told me about my mother's life – stuff I'd no idea about. Look, this sounds off the wall to me so I don't know how it must sound to you, but that's what happened. Without remembering it I was somehow . . .

A re-enactment, Dr Sugarman offered, of your mother's past?

Yes, Kurt said, relieved. Well, he said, the experience, knowing what had happened to her before I was born, left me incredibly depressed. I was sleeping all the time, which as it turns out was what she'd done, my mother, I mean, sleeping for days in this same town, having handed me over for safe-keeping to this woman, Frieda, who I met there. I have to say also that since I left Dresden and spent a lot of time alone here in New York, there's been some clarity in the process: I don't sleep all the time now and I'm putting some of the pieces together. I remember some of it easily: I know where my office is and a week ago I'd no clue. I remember the names of my co-directors, how much money I made last year – the kind of thing that a year ago was vital information and now is kinda irrelevant. Does any of this make sense to you? Anyway, when I first got to Dresden, Tennessee, I knew nothing about myself. I'd made sure of that by quitting the city. I'd no recollection of either of my parents; didn't know if I was married or divorced, the only thing I knew for sure was my name on a driver's licence. Before I got to Dresden, I'd had a few fleeting memories

177

of my mother. In Dresden, talking to her friend, more came back and later some clear memories – not the whole set – but enough to make my parents' behaviour more rational . . . Knowing what had happened to them, I mean, understanding the horror of their wartime experiences . . . But all the time I knew that something to do with *me* was lurking back there, too, in the hidden closet – something that must have set this process, this re-enactment, off in the first place . . . and I'm terrified of . . .

Of what?

That I might be mad.

Do you do mad things?

The question was so sensible that Kurt slumped with relief, No, I don't do mad things. Well, I guess I've had my mad moments.

Dr Sugarman said nothing and he had to press on alone.

I . . . I've seen things, quick, small things, images, just for a second, you know?

That's normal enough.

He began to breathe. They're like scraps of a movie, they flicker and are gone, but I sort of remember them from somewhere else, and then, like in this time with Frieda in Dresden, well, she sort of told me some things I'd already seen before she told them to me. And then I remembered bits and pieces of things that my mother did tell me that I didn't remember her telling me: terrifying things about the bombings in Germany that nobody's been saying much about for a good sixty years . . . so it's not exactly like I picked it up the way you pick up a whole lot about the Holocaust because there's so much about it, books and movies, and there's that determination that no one will forget it. It's not like that on the other side . . . there's a silence . . . And so if it's not cultural memory, it's confusing to know where the hell it's all coming from . . . even from what part of my brain . . .

It's possible, Dr Sugarman said, that your mother told you things about her life without emotion, and that way a child will not retain it.

Kurt had a sudden flash of his mother's face, averted, and was slugged by emotion. His hands shook. He dried up. For an interminable time his mind was dark and blank. The clock ticked. He was barely breathing. In the end it was the silence itself that forced him to break it; it was like an armlock, he couldn't hold out against Dr Sugarman's serene detachment, it was stronger than his rage. Anyway, he blurted out, that's not the main thing. Whether I'm crazy or not. At least, it isn't my main concern, not right now. My main concern . . . What's driving me nuts . . . And then for a horrible moment he actually thought he was going to start shouting – not at Dr Sugarman of course, but because his emotion was about to explode somewhere. The thing is this guy on the street said to me . . . and it's the real reason I'm here . . . He seemed to suggest that I had a wife . . .

You don't know this?

No. I'd forgotten everything about my life, even myself, if that makes sense. And, since meeting Hannah and being in Dresden, slowly small pieces have come in and helped me remember other things. I was beginning to recover myself quite nicely but then out of the blue . . . Well, let me back up. What happened is this: two days ago I was pursued by this guy I used to know, we worked together for a bit and sure, he knows me all right, I'd just forgotten him, along with a whole lot of other stuff I'd clearly rather not remember, which is now coming back . . . Anyway, I'm thinking now I should

179

never have come back to the city and maybe that's why I high-tailed it out of here in the first place. I'm terrified of what else is going to come creeping out of nowhere and knock me for six . . .

This agitation and anger, Mr Altmann, what is it about?

It's about whether I have a wife or not. It's about whether I have any control over my life or not . . .

How does this make you feel?

Like I want to smash someone against a wall . . . Jesus, I tell you . . . He dug his nails into his forehead and then, hearing his father's voice rapping out an order, he sat up straight and breathed out to control himself.

You sound as if you feel helpless?

Well, that's a great word, that sure is, that sums it up all right.

And the feeling that goes with the helplessness – the anger you're experiencing? It frightens you?

Kurt's body began to shake and he'd no control over that either. A small knife thrust of memory was coming at him wearing his father's face. Dr Sugarman waited for a while and then said quietly, Mr Altmann, you have some dissociated memories. The symptoms you are experiencing are tied to hidden messages which in turn are tied to unknown events. The panic and anger, the feeling of terror and losing control, these things will go down when you understand, and when the understanding is not split off from the feelings. This is the thing we are searching for – the dissociated feelings.

Great. But forgive my scepticism, when and exactly how does this happen, how do we get these dissociated feelings back? And whose feelings are they? Mine or my mother's? Can you tell me that?

Perhaps we might look at it another way? We are not

sure yet if your mother's memories have fused with your own in some way. We are not sure what else it is you need to remember. But, if you can see your return to New York and this man you met as an opportunity to remember more, perhaps it will feel less menacing? Kurt didn't respond. So, Dr Sugarman said, moving forward a fraction, If you wish to come back, next time we will try to find out if there is a wife. Kurt stared and realized that his body had gone cold. Next time? He snarled, What the hell am I supposed to do till then?

A day later he was sitting opposite Dr Sugarman again and this time the silence lasted a full five minutes. Sugarman waited patiently while Kurt studied a line of clinical degrees on the wall without being able to read any of the black letters, which took on the look of wrought iron, which then began to melt. Dr Sugarman had agreed to see him today only because Kurt had been amazingly pushy about it. And now that he was here he was watching the minutes tick by, not able to open his trap. He felt an enormous sense of relief and gratitude when Dr Sugarman spoke first. What are you feeling in this silence, Mr Altmann?

Terror, he said mildly, but it seems a long way off, not even in this room – way back in the past somewhere, but my past, not my mother's. And that man I told you about yesterday, he's the catalyst, his question makes it inevitable that I go back.

Go back where?

Even to tell you the address, he said, scares the hell out of me. Even to think of going there makes me want to bolt. In fact, that's the terror now that I come to think of it. If I run again, Hannah's not going to put up with it, but the compulsion is overwhelming and I'm not sure I can block it.

To run? Leave the city, like before?

To get as far away as I can.

What are you trying to escape?

I don't know.

Are you trying to get away from Hannah?

I don't think so. But I feel like I'm losing control again. I've started walking in that compulsive way. It's mindless. I just walk all day and I could keep going all night. I thought those days were over because once I heard about my mother's life, something let go of me. I felt normal, understood what had happened and why. I could be happy again, with Hannah, and now I'm thinking sometimes at night of bolting the way I did before. I've promised myself not to do this. I've promised her, but I've broken so many promises already. I don't trust myself with her . . .

Do you think, perhaps, you might damage her?

Why the fuck would I think that? He was furious again, wanting to punch a wall. When Kurt said nothing, Dr Sugarman said nothing.

Yes, Kurt spat out, I am likely to damage her. I sometimes feel like a suicide bomber if you really want to know.

Whom have you damaged before?

What?

Whom might you have damaged before?

Look, I don't know what you're getting at . . . are you suggesting I've killed someone? Done something terrible? There was an entirely different kind of silence in the room. Not a squeak out of Sugarman, not a breath out of Kurt. This time he was going to sit it out, wait Sugarman out, break him. But instead Dr Sugarman said, This anger of yours might feel as frightening as it does because you don't know what it might make you do. Do you remind yourself of anyone when you have this anger?

My father. He was a fucking maniac. A German bomber pilot.

So this is the connection with bombs.

Thank you. I'm leaving now.

18

I have to go back, Kurt announced over dinner. Hannah stopped pouring the water, put the jug down and rested her chin on her hand. To Dr Sugarman, you mean?

No. To my old apartment – house – whatever. He put his hand out as if to restrain her, Not that I'm not going back to Dr Sugarman, I'll make an appointment in the morning.

What did you make of him?

He knows what he's at, but he doesn't give much away. That's okay, I guess, though it seems pretty measly to be sitting there spilling my guts when he says so little and charges so much. Kurt relaxed a bit. I guess it's frustrating: it helps talking to him but the time goes so incredibly fast. I think so much my head feels like it's going to bust right open. The second session was an absolute disaster. We barely spoke, but what *was* said terrified me and I don't have a clue why, and I kind of walked out on him to give myself some puny advantage, but just as I was standing up to go, he gets up and asks me: What do you really want when you run away? And I say, I want to put the terror behind me. But no, that's not what he's after, nothing so fucking simple. So he says: But what do you *want* to happen? I still don't get it, so he says: What do you want Hannah to do? I look at him blankly because, believe me, no one in this world can make me feel quite as dim and retarded as this man can and he says, When we run away we are often wanting someone to come after us. We want to be found. That knocked the wind out of me.

Why?

Because I'd always seen myself trying to find something, not to be found.

And that's more passive, more scary?

More out of control.

Is that why you want to go back to your apartment? You've been avoiding that part of town like the plague. We haven't even talked about it in ages. She nudged him gently, What's going on? You're jumpy as hell.

He looked down and reluctantly took up a fork. I don't want to go back but there's something I need to know. I *have* to know. And there it was again – the abyss with its unthinkable fall. The panic was back. He leapt right over the abyss and landed on the other side. So, he said cheerily, tell me about your day. You saw that CEO who thinks there's some looting going on in the ranks – what happened? She looked at him quietly and almost spoke, and then stopped. He knew she was letting him off the hook and he was grateful.

I think, Hannah said, that the CEO's the rat, not his chief executives.

How'd you know?

It's an instinct. He's incredibly arrogant. Thinks he can fool anyone. That he's smarter than everyone. He comes across as a Type A guy, but he's more damaged than that. He won't follow rules, thinks they don't apply to him. He's created a situation where no one challenges him because if they try he beats them to a pulp with his rhetoric and brilliance. He keeps the bar so incredibly high few people can scale it. She stopped and looked at him. I'm not sure why we're talking about this.

It's fascinating, he said. I never thought of corporations being run by sociopaths.

It's about damage, she said. He's recreating his child-hood in some way, but he can also *do* enormous damage. Everyone is usable and expendable for him. And he's a power-liar. He brought me in because he thought he could lie to me and right now I'm letting him think he can. She looked sideways at Kurt, and filled up his glass.

So how d'you know he's lying?

A couple of things. All his execs were willing to do my interview protocol – it's a scale test that hooks out criminal traits. He refused. I thought of asking him to do a poly-graph, but he'd have passed it. She smiled. Sociopaths believe their own lies.

But, he said, how can you prove he's corrupt? How d'you know? What are the criteria?

I listen to his language, his tone, the way he is to me – that in particular – how he relates. I ask questions that he could tell the truth about, but he usually chooses to lie because it has more traction for him, gives him more options. Every intervention or relationship is essentially a power play, a use or exploitation of another person.

But, Kurt protested, if he's that ruthless isn't it because they've put him at the top to be that way?

Sure. The system, the institutional organization backs that kind of CEO. He gets unspoken consent to carry on with the illegal conduct, as long as he makes big profits without bad publicity. He's fulfilled that. But the system, in spite of the new regs, is getting more corrupt all the time, so now and then there has to be a big scapegoat or a visible one like Martha Stewart to cleanse the system. The bankruptcy sys-tem works to preserve jobs and corporate assets so the SEC and the legal systems are hitting top management very hard now. She smiled, I'm just a small part of a system that's work-ing to change corporate behaviour before there's nothing left.

But, Kurt said, listening to her like his life depended on it, if it's part of the politics all the way up, how can it change?

If he crosses too many lines, Hannah said, they'll scalp him.

What happens if he gets the feeling he can't control you?

What he can't control, he breaks, and then he moves on, simple as that. Right now he's made it seem like he's doing the right thing by bringing in a company who'll work on the inside to check there's nothing going on. At the same time he gets the skinny on everyone else.

Can you get close enough to him to really check him out?

Sure, he's a narcissist, so he likes a lot of attention. And he keeps me close because he has to gauge what I'm thinking and feeling every moment – he's good at that. She looked directly at Kurt, The flaw in all this is that working with him turns me into a liar: I'm not telling him what I'm thinking.

How d'you do this kinda thing?

By getting physically close to him. I ask him certain questions and see how his body responds: his respiration, his body heat, that kind of thing. He has little or no anxiety because he has no feeling. She turned on him. Why're you asking me all these questions, anyway?

He poured her a little more wine. I want to know how you know.

She stared at him, It's not so hard: I watch him, I smell him, I check his breathing. He doesn't sweat, but I can get very accurate readings on my galvanized skin response monitor. I scrutinize his micro-expressions, his evasions and sentence constructions. He has these crazy black eyebrows and he has no idea how eloquent they are. It's sad, really, she said, because he's emotionally dead, nothing shocks or touches him. The scandals excite him, he knows all the details of the trials and can anticipate if the jury's crooked or if the results have been fixed or what muscle the state and federal regulators will pull. But if I showed him pictures of atrocities, the things that would make you or me throw up, he wouldn't respond at all. She gave a war-weary smile. And, she said, on this kind of man – nearly always male, just like serial killers – sorry about that – the corporate world thrives and prospers. You must know lots of men like John: superficially charming, quick, glib, witty and urbane, but if you look hard, they have that thousand-yard stare. There's no one home. No connection. She smiled at him. Aren't you glad you're out of all that? She said it with a small, puzzled smile, placing her hand on his wrist, as if checking his heart-rate.

God, Kurt said, getting abruptly up from the table and pacing about. I can't help feeling sorry for the poor bastard.

She turned in her chair to face him. Why's that?

Because I'm a liar too. And to tell you the truth, Hannah, I sometimes think I've done something sketchy or immoral back there. I have a sense of unease, guilt, when I hear people talking about business transactions, corporate scandals, it sends me into a panic.

She looked at him and took his hand. It's okay, she said. I checked you out, you're clean.

19

Dr Sugarman was wearing a grey suit with a dull tie, as if he didn't want to give himself away, but all the same he was smiling, his eyes surprisingly blue.

I need to talk, Kurt said, about the wife issue. It's getting more creepy all the time. Dr Sugarman nodded. At first, I used to get images of a woman who was with me in some way, then I'd lose them again. The other day, after the guy yelled out Elizabeth, the images sort of lined up. That name, by the way, has been around for a bit in odd ways: a hooker in a bar said her name was Elizabeth, I saw the name on a plaque in St Bart's and it rattled me enough to make me run out of there, and then the guy on the street yelled it at me.

So, Mr Altmann, he said, there is an Elizabeth in your life but you have no recall of her.

No. But I feel guilty about this woman, as if I'm betraying her.

With Hannah?

Correct. It's like I've forgotten a significant woman in my past and the only feeling that's attached to her is guilt. Guilt has been following me for months. I thought once I might be a terrorist or a suicide bomber or some other maniac. When I read about bombings in Iraq or Pakistan I took them personally, I felt involved. I began to think I'd been part of some corporate corruption, but that isn't true either. So now I'm wondering if the guilt's personal and I've just been projecting it out there? Hannah says it might be connected to some kind of appropriation of German guilt. Are Germans still guilty or can they be innocent now?

Dr Sugarman smiled. If they can't that would make you guilty. And your mother. And me, too, even though I'm Jewish. The question is, can Germans be forgiven? Can the Japanese, British, Americans be forgiven? Can the Islamic bombers or the Israelis? Can Bush or Cheyne be forgiven? Who is guilty, who is not guilty?

My mother was too young to be guilty. She was fourteen.

You defend her. Why do you need to?

What are you getting at?

Perhaps the woman you feel guilty about is your mother. You told me she's dead. This caused you great pain when Frieda told you. How do you feel about her death right now? Kurt felt his throat close up. Perhaps, Dr Sugarman said, you feel guilty about her death? Kurt got up and was heading for the door. Stay, Dr Sugarman said. Stop the running. Let's look at this. Kurt was at the window, looking up at the sky. There was a long silence. Come, sit, Dr Sugarman said. He waited a moment longer and then said, Your mother's name was Else? Pretty close to Elizabeth.

Close enough.

Tell me what you remember about her death.

She had a stroke.

Tell me what happened.

Kurt crossed the room and sat back in his chair. His voice was low and flat. She'd been sick for a while. Had one minor stroke and recovered. She had this problem . . . He blew his breath out . . . This problem with breathing. They said her lungs had been damaged, probably some kind of smoke . . . He looked away and said, Right now, I can't breathe . . . I feel like I'm suffocating . . .

This is part of the past. You've made a connection with it, that's all. It's not actually happening.

I'm thinking about that book, *The Stranger*. And how the son goes to see his mother after she died in that institution. He's a cold fucking bastard, I remember the first line of the book – something about his not remembering which day his mother died, today or yesterday. It was unimportant to him . . .

How did it affect you at the time?

It made me mad.

Did you have that feeling about your mother's death?

Kurt looked up angrily. Who d'you think I am? I loved my mother. I took care of her in the years before she died. I remembered her illness, her way of seeming to have no feeling – her death. I remembered it after Frieda told me.

And the character in the book?

He was . . . a sociopath . . . I guess . . . No feelings . . . There was a long silence.

When a mother dies we feel abandoned, Dr Sugarman said, and angry.

It wasn't her fault, Kurt said, his voice breaking. None of it was her fault, the way she was, the things she did. I didn't know then what made her so, so . . .

So what?

So cold. He took a deep breath. But I didn't get there in time. I wasn't with her . . . No one was with her . . . He looked across the gap. Dr Sugarman said quietly, Perhaps that is the way she wanted it?

Perhaps it's the way I wanted it.

Hannah took his arm and they walked across Park Avenue. Thanks for coming, he said, I'm sorry I've been a bit out of it lately. This stuff takes a lot out of me. They

191

walked in silence for a while as he told her about his mother. We could find the place, she said. We could go back and see where she's buried. I know where it is, he said. I went there for years, every week, on a Tuesday. I was never sure she recognized me, or gave a damn if I was there or not. He's right, of course, Dr Sugarman, there's a lot I want to forget about her, the way she was as a mother. When she slipped into that twilight place she was unreachable – gone. He turned to Hannah. The wind was cold and he reached across to pull up the collar of her jacket. She tipped her face to kiss his hand. Before I look at her grave, he said, I first need to find out where I lived. I remember her funeral. Frieda came with me. It was just the two of us. It was very windy. She died on May 8th. We buried her in the grounds of the institution and Frieda cried a lot more than I did. I had very little feeling. I loved her, but it was a desperate, helpless kind of love and I didn't know what to do with it once she'd died. Perhaps, Hannah said, it was always a bit like that with her, when you were little, a helpless looking at her without knowing what to do. And now, she said, It's more urgent to go home first? He was walking very fast and she stopped. Can you try to slow down a bit? He walked back to her. This is a lot to take in all at once, she said. Perhaps wait a bit . . . We could go away for a few days, leave the city?

The next day he was back at Dr Sugarman's. It had become the only place, bar the apartment, where he felt safe. Earlier that day he'd called in a panic to make an appointment only to get Dr Sugarman's voicemail: Leave a message and I will get back to you today. The 'today' gave him some relief, and after he'd pulled himself together, he'd gone home in a cab and sat next to the phone watching the hours jerk slowly round the clock. When the phone rang he sprang up like a sentry, answered it, spoke briefly into it, and went down to get a cab. Dr Sugarman saw him immediately.

It's happening again, Kurt said. He looked at Dr Sugarman, trying to read his expression, trying to see if he cared. And there was something about him that seemed softer and, since it was 6.30, and the man was obviously going out of his way to accommodate him, the wind at his back died down a bit. Thank you for seeing me, he said, I really appreciate it.

I was down in Lower Manhattan, he said, having lunch with Hannah. I wanted to tell her about the Elizabeth situation, and I needed neutral ground. His voice was racing and he could feel his heart crashing around in his ribcage like a hooked fish. Anyway, after lunch I started walking and I guess I walked a long way, up past the public library and St Patrick's, and while I was in there I saw a man who was wearing a thick neck-bandage and large round glasses, his mouth was flopped open all the time and his bottom lip had been severed and stitched down the middle. There was this dark red scar down his chin, and the rest of his face looked melted, it was white and waxy with skin that swirled and rippled as if someone had stirred it with a spoon. And I saw a boy outside Dunhills sitting close to the curb with his body slumped forward and his head on the sidewalk and I didn't know if he was dead or alive but I walked right past him like everyone else. I saw people covered in blankets who'd crawled into corners and there were buildings without sides or backs and gutted windows in blackened walls and dust and rubble was falling down onto Fifth Avenue and I saw all those slowly furling

193

flags everywhere and I thought, why am I seeing all this
and then I had a sudden shocking question: Have we ever
said *we're* sorry? Have *we* ever asked to be forgiven for our
crimes?

I kept walking and I was doing okay because I remembered everything, just as before. There was no amnesia. I
saw square umbrellas in Aspreys and a London taxi
behind a yellow cab, and a new black Rolls Royce and
another and then a third and everywhere a profusion of
magnolias and of course the Plaza, and I kept on past the
statue, *In Memoriam, 1918*, and cut across the park which
was green and busting out with blossom but by now my
mind's gone blank. Up ahead of me I see the elegant twin
towers of the pale San Remo Buildings, the narrow windows blue as the sky, incredibly beautiful with the ornate
Victorian spires and it sort of dazes me and then I come to
the turrets of a Germanic-looking building on Central Park
West and I get a bit fixated on that and I keep staring at it a
long time until I think maybe I'm arousing suspicion, you
know how you can't hang around outside a building too
long without being interrogated? And that reminds me of
a time at the airport when I made a stupid joke and before
I know it I'm in with the security people and they keep me
there for hours while they check me out and ask me exactly what I've been doing for the last ten years of my life. I
turn the corner and I'm looking at the Dakota Building
with its half-moon extensions that jut out and the small
blue domes and the windows are blue and the sky is too
and I'm staring up at those triangular Teutonic peaks and
crenellations and the heavy carved masonry, all so perfect
and intact, and then I remember John Lennon got shot
there. And that's it. That's the last thing I remember. After
that, nothing. I'm walking and I'm crossing Columbus,

194

nothing, Amsterdam, nothing. Everything's strange and unreal. I go past a red-brick parking garage with its windows blown out and now I'm completely disorientated because I think I'm in Germany, but all around me Americans are rushing about. I'm reading the name Broadway like I've never seen it before. I start sweating and I'm walking like someone's dragging me and I'm feeling such panic I can't tell you but I keep putting one foot in front of the other because I don't know what else to do and I haven't the first idea where I am but I sure as hell don't think I've ever seen this place or even this country before.

Kurt took a breath and kept on, talking very rapidly, as if he was following some kind of map. And then I'm in a leafy street, five-storey buildings all lined up close together and now my breathing's short and shallow and it's like I'll pass out. I stop and gulp in air and I look up at a brownstone building and these windows are blue too and they seem to be about to fall out and I'm staring at the steps up to the door, there's a black trash-bag on the curb and I want to go up to the door but I'm stuck, my mouth gaping, my lungs mangled by terror. I don't want to know what's in the black bag. I've dreamed this and this house has dreamed me. I stop dead and look at the outside door which is open, showing the inner door, and I look up at the fan-shaped glass above the door where the numbers say 102 and I brake. This is my house. This is where I live. At that moment I know this is where Elizabeth lives too. My panic is so overwhelming that I start to run. I try to make myself go back, go back, but don't run because if you run they'll shoot you in the back. Go up the stairs and go in. Do it. But then I realize I don't have the keys. I want to scream with gratitude and relief, and the panic goes down but not entirely because unfortunately I know where the keys are. The last time I saw them was in Memphis when I tipped out my bag before leaving Hannah at two in the morning that first time. There's a different bolt on this memory but when it slides back I see they're still in my bag, in the pocket with a zipper. That's when I got out of there and it was only when I was far enough away from that neighbourhood that all the buildings and streets came sailing back into memory and I knew where I was again. I could think and walk normally and that's when I called you . . . I can't imagine what I'd have done if you couldn't have seen me . . .

He stopped, breathless and shaken.

Can I get you a glass of water, Mr Altmann?

Please.

Dr Sugarman returned and gave it to him and laid his hand lightly on Kurt's shoulder before returning to his seat five feet away. Kurt dropped his head into his hands and began to press his fingers into his neck muscles.

Dr Sugarman looked at him, his eyes war-weary.

Kurt looked up. I'm seeing things differently, he said, and I don't like it. New York looks different to me. I don't feel so proud of being American any more. I don't feel too good about being me any more either.

He wanted to go back to before, before the walk across the park to the San Remo Buildings, before the Dakota Building, before his unopened house, before Dr Sugarman, he wanted to go back to the early part of the day when he was sitting next to Hannah in Lower Manhattan, eating seafood pasta and laughing. She'd taken his hand and studied his life-line, which was long and uninterrupted, and kissed his palm and said, It feels a bit like the time just before you told me there was no head injury. Remember that? Why's it feeling that way? He sat up straight, You're right. It's another lie. Something I've kept from you and I'm really sorry.

She stared at him.

I stumbled across something . . . and I should have told you the minute it happened, but I wanted you to guess, or to ask me, which is pathetic. Sometimes I thought you knew . . .

I think you tried to tell me last night – but I didn't take you up on it. I was afraid of what you'd say. I kept going full blast on corporate fraud and lying . . . to stop you telling me. Her hand had wandered off on its own and he returned it to his. I'm sorry, I really am, he said. I knew what you were doing. I should have told you right then. He took a deep breath, I met a banker on Park Avenue a couple of days ago – he and I talked a bit – and at the end, when he was walking away, he turned and said, Say hullo to Elizabeth for me.

Elizabeth?

Elizabeth.

Elizabeth who?

My impression was she must be a wife or partner or . . .

Yours?

I guess.

Your wife or partner?

I don't know. The whole thing feels like a fucking disaster area . . .

Her hand crashed down on the table and it shook violently, the knives rushed for cover, the waiter jumped. The eyes of the lunchers, having hovered just long enough on Hannah to infuriate her, swivelled back to their plates.

Thanks, she said, for sparing me two days of hell. Her

head was down and her curls were shaggy and forlorn, curvaceous and beautiful, all at the same time. He felt something cold and reptilian go out between them, an insidious little snake that was slithering so fast he couldn't stop it. He saw her hand tremble as she plucked furiously at her pink napkin. He reached over and covered it, holding it still. He leaned across and kissed her mouth which was white. I'm so sorry, he said. Her teeth were fastening her top lip to the lower one to button her tongue. When she'd calmed herself down, she looked at him and said, How did you think I'd be?

The way you are.

Did you think I wouldn't understand?

I didn't think I could expect that.

Did you think I wouldn't love you enough to help you with this?

He stared at her, and pressed his eyes with his forefinger and thumb, and then looked directly into hers. I'm not sure how you could love a man who doesn't really know who he is or whether he's free to marry you or not.

Well I do love you. And I'm still not holding you responsible for what you don't know. But – she glared at him – you most definitely should have told me.

You're absolutely right. The waiter sailed in with two new glasses and poured a dash of wine into each, whisking away debris like a magician, covering the wine stain with a starched napkin, and offering a dessert menu. The restaurant breathed out and the lunchers began to eat again. Life went on its merry way.

I suppose, Hannah said, we'll see now whether we can resist tearing one another to shreds or not. But, she said, I need to know who Elizabeth is. I need to know. I don't care what it is, how bad it is, I need to know, and most of all I don't want to hear that I'm not being told because you don't want to hurt me. That's bullshit. Every lie is told to get some personal advantage. And you need to shine the same light on me because I'm just as capable of deception. Her voice tipped. I feel empty-handed, she said, and I'd like to resist hurting you or getting hurt. Do you think we might possibly pull that off? She turned and looked directly into his eyes. It feels like adultery, she said, and I won't do that again.

His voice was steady and calm. We don't know who Elizabeth is, he said, perhaps she was a woman I lived with and we broke up and that's why I left . . .

Is that what you think or what you feel?

It's what I think. I feel nothing about Elizabeth. But I know what to do about it. He caught the waiter's attention and the check came in a flash. She slid her hand across his bare arm. Do you want me to come with you, she asked, or would you rather go alone?

Mr Altmann, Dr Sugarman said, you have been silent for seven minutes. Can you tell me where you've been?

I'm sorry, he said. I was thinking about before – earlier. And I'm ashamed to tell that when I got to my house I chickened out. I didn't have the keys so I left and called you and went home.

You are mighty tough with yourself, Dr Sugarman said. You were buying a little time, that's all.

My father wouldn't have seen it that way.

Ah, the father.

With him you got it right the first time.

I see. So, your father, he is here with us now. Tell me about him.

Nutcase. Anger high as the house. No control. The failure of the war destroyed him. He took it personally. He said to me that he should have shot himself when Germany surrendered, that his superior officers shot themselves and he wasn't a man because he failed to do the same. And, that way, of course, I wouldn't have been born. In one way I've been running from that all my life.

So, now: if you stop running, what will happen?

Kurt looked up. If I don't run, I'll die. He was silent a long time. He didn't look at Dr Sugarman and he felt awkward, wanting to leave. Finally, Dr Sugarman said, I think right now you may be having some feelings about us.

Us?

You and me.

You and *me*? How you and me?

There are two of us here and I am an older man, a father figure. When you go silent I think you might be troubled about something to do with the relationship between the two of us.

In what way?

Perhaps it has something to do with the fact that you are a German and I a Jew?

Kurt's eyes flared. Dr Sugarman, he said, my personal history is not frozen in death camps or burned in ovens. I come from a line of the guilty.

Dr Sugarman shrugged. Isn't it a cycle of defeat and humiliation leading to a re-enactment of the same: the defeat of Germany in the First World War led to the Second; the defeat of the US at 9/11 led to Iraq and Iraq will keep coming back to us in new forms of violence. So who is guilty?

Another three minutes of silence. Dr Sugarman said: We have only two choices, to close down in rage and numbness or open up to transformation and change.

Thank you, Kurt said, that helps me. He waited a moment before he said, I'd like to ask you a personal favour . . . The testimony my mother wrote about the war, about Dresden . . . I wondered if you'd read it?

Can you tell me why you'd like this?

Can we not fucking analyse everything I say? Sometimes it feels like an interrogation.

Dr Sugarman nodded. Bring it next time.

It was late, about nine, when Kurt got back to Prince Street, and when he got to the apartment he could hear a solo violin. Hannah was in the middle of the room, wearing a black leotard and pink soft shoes, no points, no tights, and her muscly body gleamed as her feet came down on the bare boards with a steady thud, thud, thud. When her arms fell and she saw him, she hesitated, and in her uncertainty he felt the ache of a lost illusion. She stepped over it and came toward him, her arms clearing the air as if shovelling cobwebs. Through the windy spaces of the open skylights snaps of music – African, Indian, Spanish – flew up into the loft like street birds dashing for cover, and this music, raw and loud, changed the space again. He went quickly to her and, for a moment, her head collapsed on his shoulder. I thought you'd never get here, she said, I came home early to see you. She put her arms around him and for a moment he let himself be held and comforted. She began to talk softly to him and she was so serene that he wondered about it. He had the strongest sense that she'd gone to his apartment, ahead of him, and was waiting for him to find out what she already knew.

When Kurt saw Dr Sugarman, the sheath of his mother's papers, which he'd left the session before, was on the circular table next to his chair. He sat down and tried not to look at them. Burned edges moved a little in the breeze coming from the window and made a rustling sound. After a few minutes had sped by, he looked at Dr Sugarman, D'you see anything weird about these papers?

No.

Well, a minute ago they were burning, little flames at the edges. That's gotta be pathological, right?

Not necessarily.

How so?

Well, if you were telling me you could actually see them burning you'd be having some kind of psychotic break. But what I think you're telling me is that it's an image in your mind?

It's quite real in my mind.

Of course. Do you smell fire?

I have at times.

Tell me about that.

Well, after I read this, Kurt glanced nervously at the pages, I suppose I was in a trance . . . and I saw . . . and, this is what confuses me: to say I saw is too literal, it's just what I *experienced*. Heat was running all over my body and I couldn't breathe. I began to panic. Well . . . it felt as though there was a weight on my chest, that I was carrying something . . .

It's all right, Kurt, Dr Sugarman said calmly, you're not having a heart attack. Just tell me what you saw.

I saw bodies being sucked into a vortex, hundreds of them blown and tossed about in the air before being incinerated in a burning crater.

You were seeing this, or did you feel that you were there?

Both.

There was a silence in which Kurt began to feel dizzy again.

This scene, Dr Sugarman said, is described in your mother's document: she was writing about a direct hit by the Allies, the British and the American bomber pilots who dropped high-explosive bombs, weighing over four thousand pounds, and incendiary bombs that created vast craters and fires that rose high into the sky, pulling in oxygen and spinning the air currents until they reached hurricane force. The fires kept on burning, setting the canals on fire, melting glass and asphalt, melting bodies . . . The ground was hot and steaming for months . . . Did you know about this – about what happened to German cities in fire-storms?

If you're asking if I knew about what I was reading in my mother's account, the answer's no. I'd not come across that information before. But there's something, Kurt said, that isn't clear: I was holding something and it was ripped away from me . . . And I've never felt such pain and loss, such complete devastation. I was carrying something, I was responsible for it and I couldn't hold onto it . . .

I'm wondering, Dr Sugarman said, if these feelings are to do with some memory of your own?

Something I've forgotten?

Possibly.

But what's that got to do with whatever my mother was

describing all those years ago.

Dr Sugarman said, There is something that is not explained in your mother's description. Did you notice that?

No.

Well, did you wonder what had happened to her brother? Rudi? Did you notice how he disappears from the text?

That same night, sleepless, the usual hour shoved him out of the sheets and into the cool air of the bedroom. Hannah was asleep, arms and legs flung about and as his body remembered her that way, it lifted and hardened. His eyes wandered over her breasts and slid down the straight lines of her hips and legs and up again to her belly where he'd planted her, he was sure that in the dark safety of her womb a bud was putting on cells, multiplying with life. He walked to the windows, listening to the far drone of a plane in the sky, but it was still too early. Flung over a chair was a new dress he'd bought her before all this pandemonium started up. It was made of soft broken linen, the palest blue, strapless, with a skirt that fell into wide pleats. He picked it up, felt the fabric and located the safety pin he'd used to mark the right length and went to where the sewing things were kept, in a straw Ethiopian basket on the top shelf of the closet behind the bookshelf. He pressed the lever and entered the hiding place, watching the bookshelf disappear into the wall. It was dark and a little frightening in there – what if, say, the lever failed or the air ran out? He wondered if she'd ever closed herself in and, as he thought about Hannah's grandmother, he remembered Dr Sugarman's words: There's an unbreakable thread between second-generational children and survivors, between Hitler's grandchildren and the dead. They are the one who will carry us forward.

When he stepped out and into the bedroom, Hannah stirred and sat up, resting her chin in her hand: Did you just lock yourself in there?

Only for a very short time.

You're a lunatic, know that?

I do.

I suppose, she said, it must be two in the morning?

Closer to three.

You've been awake a whole hour? Take an Ambien like the rest of us.

I slept for three hours and that's enough. My mind speeds at night – takes me to interesting places. He walked over. Did you ever ask your grandmother about her time in the closet in Hamburg?

Sure, and she said to me, Why would I remember a time when I was out of my mind and everyone was dead?

Why did you make it?

I don't really know: it wasn't a bunker to escape to – what good would a bunker do with the bombs we have? It's more a tribute to her, a memorial of sorts. You're the only person who knows about it. She slid her hand across the sheet the way she caressed his shoulders and arms and, looking up, eyes fragile and bright, she said, There's a second hiding place in there, behind the partition wall.

What's in it?

Her violin. And some other stuff my mom was chucking in the trash when my grandmother died. She hesitated, I did spend some hours in there, once. He moved till he was resting against her side, making a wall. I did a painting, she said, a bouquet of barbed wire and roses, with her number, the one on her arm, tangled up in the wire. She looked down, I used to run my finger along the outline when I was

205

a kid. She told me she'd burned that arm shovelling hot coals and they put the numbers on top of the burn.

When she was asleep, he walked to the closet and pushed the lever: the bookcase returned with the books in long lines, straight as soldiers. Walking back to the table where the reading lamp made its halo, he slipped the blue dress off its hanger and arranged it flat on the floor, and in that moment a voice leapt out of the air: Don't. Don't. Your hands are too big, you're hurting him, you'll break his ribs . . . Let me . . . five compressions, two breaths . . . alternating . . . Yes, I know . . . third and fourth fingers . . . I *know* . . . a hundred a minute . . . Put the speaker-phone on . . . Keep talking to her . . . I can't . . . Tell me again . . . okay . . . no . . . don't . . . He picked up the scissors and began to cut the hem in a dead straight line, using the length he'd cut as a ruler to guide him the rest of the way. He sat on the chair under the light and stitched bias-binding onto the cut edge and when that was done he turned it under to make a hem. He stitched carefully, so only the smallest nicks showed through the linen and when it was done there was nothing on the outside to show, no imprint of needle, no slash of thread. As he hung it back on its satin hanger he was wondering where he might take her the first time she wore it – perhaps to go dancing? He remembered how they'd danced in Memphis, and how he'd felt holding her, brand new feelings, exquisite and fragile, and how, looking into her eyes and face, something between them had gone too deep for words. He shut off the light and sat still, not thinking, not feeling. He was only waiting: for the pigeons to settle on the windowsills, for the moon to slide over the asphalt and illuminate the skyscrapers; for the city to rise out of darkness and return to life. Then it would be time to go. Only this time it wouldn't be the loneliness of long distance, it would be a slow steady march all the way home.

Dearest Hannah, since you were kind enough to say, yes, I'm going back to see if I can marry you.

As Kurt walked through the park at dawn, slim young males let slip one another's hands and headed off home as other shadowy figures came creeping out the bushes, shaking off the twigs and damp of a night spent on the ground. One of the apparitions, in dark layers of matted cloth, and wearing a bandage on one foot, shuffled up to ask Kurt for money.

What happened to your foot?

Got hurt in the war.

Which one?

One still going on. One we were going to win in a week. Right? Shock and awe. I got it in the foot. He grinned, showing a grim set of teeth.

What's the money for?

Food and survival.

How much d'you need?

If you can spare thirty, I'd go downtown and cop some crack to take the pain away.

What would you do with a hundred?

Buy more crack.

Here's thirty. Save some for a sandwich.

When Kurt reached the end of the park, he sat for a moment on the benches of Strawberry Fields and read the messages to the dead, and as he crossed over Central Park West the windows of the Dakota Building were no longer blue, nor the domes nor the sky, everything was grey as if

charred. It was quiet as he stood looking up, half-expect-
ing his memory to break up again the way it had the day
before. He looked across at the doorway where Lennon
had died and in that moment he was consumed by grief,
wave after wave, images scattering like mercury on stone:
a blue blanket, feet racing up stairs, thud, thud, thud, a
jump-bag, an oxygen canister . . . a door . . . a woman huddled over . . . a baby lying on the rug . . . a woman frantic
with fear . . . her howl as a paramedic shoved her aside . . .
How long? . . . When did you last look in? . . . How old? . . .
Miss, could you please move . . . And the same motions . . .
the small face bouncing on the rug . . . Kurt retreated,
pressing his back against a wall, looking not across at the
Dakota Building but down at the sidewalk. He'd been
warned by Dr Sugarman: beneath the memory is the pain.
Be careful. But it was too late, the flares were lined up, the
target was inside him now, the bomb ready to blow. He
forced himself to keep walking. He remembered the Italian
restaurant on the left, and the Ossobuco in Bianco and
when he crossed Columbus, he remembered it too, and his
dry-cleaner next to Starbucks. Amsterdam was all clear,
and the red-brick parking garage with blown-out windows, all clear too. By now he was sweating profusely.
Stores were opening, flowers blooming in steel tubs, coffee
brewing, cafés and coffee shops opening to take in crates
of bagels and tomatoes, the sounds of trucks slowing to
slap down newspapers, the windy sounds of bus brakes. A
lone bicyclist was tooling through as night-traders headed
home, and through the open doors of a hotel he heard the
gathering hum of vacuum cleaners as they merged with
the drone of taxis and sirens in the distance. The sky was
pale, a faint pink on the far horizon. He heard a bird, and
then another. He walked faster, trying to outwalk the

shakes, and by the time he reached the newly leafed street with its five-storey brownstones he was panting. He stepped over black trash bags drenched in dew, and then his body buckled. He put his hands on his knees and blew out air, gulped back oxygen, panting, but soon, like a soldier, he straightened up to his father's voice: Be a man, behave like a man. He walked into the cold early morning wind, feeling in his jacket the icy block of his keys.

Standing outside his brownstone, he felt in his pocket for his keys. He held the bigger of the two for a minute, hesitating before pushing the key in the lock; the door swung open as if someone had pulled it from inside. He stepped into the hallway onto a mosaic of yellow and blue tiles. He gasped. The stench was abominable. He reeled, putting his hand across his nose and mouth, stepping over a deep pile of envelopes, Fed-Ex packets, circulars and unpaid bills. He rushed into the room on the right, slamming the door on the stench and throwing up the windows. Air rushed in and when he could breathe normally again he turned slowly to look around him. He remembered the room as if he'd never mislaid it. He was home. His eyes took in the pale carpets, the rosy walls and sofas with scarlet cushions, the piles of books, the white orchids in brass urns, petals papery and dead, the newspaper with its date: January 7, 2006. There was a dining room on the other side of the connecting doors. For a moment he felt calm, as if a circle was closing and, as he came back to himself, he went to call Hannah. The phone had been disconnected. He stared at the receiver and replaced it, and went back out into the hallway and pushed through the polluted air into the kitchen where, grabbing a trash bag from the top drawer, he flung open the fridge door and instantly retreated to the sink to vomit. He found a dishcloth and wet it, placing it over his nose and mouth, and went back to the fridge and began digging through the carnage of decomposed chicken and putrefied milk, rotting vegetables, slimed salads, cheese and butter crawling with gangrene, potatoes sprouting tumours, everything rank and malodorous and dead. He raked everything into the bag, watching the soft pulpy flesh slide down the sides before settling into postures of repose: a bottle curled into the side of a cabbage, a tomato bled onto the crushed limbs of celery, swollen cartons and broken bones shifted one last time until the sides of the pit closed in around them. Coming up for air, he grabbed a roll of paper towel and wiped his hands clean, then, like a man about to drop from the sky, he took one last breath and fought his way through the rest of the debris and rubble until bottles, cans, plastic containers, mildewed soup, dead cheese, atrophied rice and noodles, loose flying eggs and heels of bread were all buried in the sack where they stirred and settled and lay still. He tied the ends and dragged the bag across the tiles and bumped it down the steps to the kerb. The door whammed shut behind him. His head flew back in panic. He let go of the bag and grovelled through his pockets for his keys. They were still in the door.

The kitchen window was open, and a sweet cloying smell struggled with the ammonia in the sink. He held his hands under the tap in the sink until the water ran out with a dry rattle. He felt nothing, no irritation, no panic. He merely filled another bag with the heaps of stained and sodden paper towels until all that was left was a bottle of champagne with a yellow label. Friends were milling around in the kitchen, the sunlight landed on gifts, on chairs, and wandered over to a pile of coats piled high in the corner. There was jazz playing, champagne pouring into tall flutes and Elizabeth was standing by the window, holding a baby on her hip and trying, with her other hand, to cut a christening cake. He took out the champagne, cleaned it, and put it back into the body of the fridge. The door shut with a whisper and he wondered why the fridge alarm wasn't going off the way it should, but of course the electricity had been cut off. There was nothing to wash his hands with now. He took the champagne out, prised off the cork with his teeth, and turning his eyes from the explosion, poured froth over his hands, watching the bubbles drain away, leaving the porcelain white and empty.

Now he didn't want to leave the kitchen, couldn't leave it, hadn't the faintest intention of leaving it. The last of the fetid smell slowly wafted out the window and mingled with the plants in the window box. They were alive and going about their business, putting on new shoots, producing buds and curled leaves, waiting for the sunshine to come round to that side of the wall. He sat on the floor with his head flopped forward until a martial voice said Go, Go, Go, and he got up as if kicked. He walked back into the hallway where he stood looking up the stairs that led to the sleeping floor, where the three white doors in his dreams were waiting to be opened. He crouched on the floor with his body in a lock and held on fast, not moving. An hour passed. And another. He watched time fall like petals from the centre of a peony, one by one, until there was only a stem.

He walked up the stairs, one foot in front of the other. A paramedic was running up two by two . . . shoving him out of the way . . . crouching down . . . five to two, 100 per minute . . . questions strafing the air: How long? . . . fifteen seconds? How long when? . . . Can you please? . . . NO . . . Keep trying . . . you have to . . . please . . . don't, don't stop . . . Okay . . . yes, I see . . . intubation? What vein? . . . His weight? . . . Epinephrine? . . . Will it work . . . why not? . . . Oh God, oh God, oh God . . . NO . . . Try that . . . just try it . . . manually . . . I see, yes . . . Can I hold him? . . . Miss, can you please move aside . . . We're putting him on the board . . . the ambulance . . . just you . . . your husband will have to go in the police car . . . Don't . . . don't . . . for God's sake don't . . . Miss, you need to let go . . . Okay, okay . . . On the stairs there's a blue baby sock falling . . . and feet going thud, thud, thud . . . she's holding the blue blanket . . . flashing lights and the freezing cold, the cop car . . . a man turning to look back. He climbed one more step, trying to breathe as his lungs flooded . . . Up ahead on the landing a woman was pulling her hair, and seeing her there, seeing the way her face began to blur, it was as if the skin of a pre- vious soul left him, and he slid down in front of the closed door and stopped dead. All that was left was a ghost of regret, a sorrow knowing no bounds. He knew what had taken place at the top of the stairs, in the rooms of the first floor, behind the white door, unalterable now . . .

The weight against his chest was unbearably heavy now . . . He wanted to scream: Where's Rudi? Who was hold- ing Rudi? The weight was ripped out of his arms. Girls' skirts were ballooning in the sky . . . legs falling through air . . . twisting in spirals of heat . . . hair on fire . . . hands in the furnace reaching out for Rudi . . . Come, baby, come . . . He slumped down on the carpet, his muscles weak as a girl's. He stayed there motionless for a long while until a shadow reached in from the window in the

212

hall below, and the sound of workmen on the street woke him: snatches of music on the radio, Tracy Chapman singing 'Give Me One Reason', blare of horns, pit of silence, small blue face in a matching wool hat, nose and mouth making pools of shadow, mask without a pulse. Ben's cot was in the corner, away from the window, at his heels the dimpled chaise where his mother slept when he was born, to nurse him, to check he was breathing . . . Elizabeth sitting on the floor with piles of baby clothes and you know how you get these bigger clothes that the baby will grow into . . . She was folding the clothes that Ben wasn't going to grow into. She was putting them in boxes that she tied with blue silk ribbon. What am I doing? What d'you think I'm doing? I'm distracting myself, can't you let me be just for a minute so I can go back? He said, It's cold in here, couldn't you come and do that in the study? Here, let me help you. She said, I can't leave the crib. He asked her again, Can't you just try? Elizabeth . . . you have to come out of here . . . it's over a month . . . I can't, she said, so go . . . just go . . . I need to stay in case he comes back.

Upstairs, in the room with the crib he felt an emptiness that was physical. At the window looking out at the snow, the weight of Rudi against him and the smell of damp and wool, the weight of him – Ben not Rudi – and the lullaby, was it Brahms? His mother's song that he used to sing to Ben: *Go to sleep, do not stir, for the angels are near, they will rock you in their arms* . . . He walked into his study next door and sat down at his desk. The things of the house were breathing, he knew them, they were dear to him because they proved he'd once lived here, that there'd been life here once. Each object had a connection to him, the blue

213

cover on the bed, the clock that had fallen and smashed the picture, the books along the wall facing his desk, the bottom stair where she put on her shoes to go running, the stove where the soup boiled on winter evenings, the black pram in a closet waiting to be pushed in the park, the photos buried in dust . . . He looked through the drawers, his name kept cropping up, endlessly, on the left hand side of documents, reams of paper, statements, financial records, letters, on and on.

On the chair covered in pale yellow suede which bore the imprint of his body was a small pile of documents. I put them there before I began walking, I must have known I'd come back. At the moment of my leaving I can honestly tell you I'd no intention of coming back to these rooms and all that happened here. These are the papers that hold the facts but right now I can't face them. He rubbed his eyes to dislodge an image: he was walking with Elizabeth by the sea, it was cold, perhaps a mistake to come, too soon, but at least he'd got her out of the house. It was Sunday, they'd had lunch in a fish restaurant and though she'd been very quiet, she seemed a little less shattered. He was telling her that they could go away, somewhere warm, try to get pregnant again. Too soon. He'd held her hands and tried to comfort her. The word, inconsolable, came to him. He stood at the window and looked down at the street. In that instant he could feel Hannah coming to him. It was the way he'd known she was coming to Dresden. Once she was here things would settle. He'd stop running. Perhaps she'd already come? Perhaps she'd already found the name next to his: Lazard, Elizabeth Lazard. A name full of money. He went back to the desk and, picking up a pen, opened a pad of yellow legal paper and started to write, very fast, on and on writing, as if running for his life.

Elizabeth went in the ambulance and I watched her climb in and sit opposite Ben, leaning forward, her dark hair over her face. He looked dead. That's just the way he looked. I reached out to her before they closed the doors but she was looking straight ahead. I walked away and went with the cop. He was asking questions and telling me there'd be an investigation by the police and the medical examiner's office: standard procedure following an unexpected death in the home. I got out and took a cab to the hospital. One more question and I'd have broken his jaw. The panic and noise of ER. They're trying for our sakes to make it seem like there's a chance. Doing all the same procedures one more time. Elizabeth's a ghost. I'm answering the questions the paramedic's already asked, but I'll answer them again: Four months and eight days. Full-term. 8 pounds, 1 oz. Breast fed. Yes. Before he was put down for the night. On his back. Yes, of course, no pillow, no obstructions, of course he never stopped breathing before. No. Through the corner of my eye I can see the doctor working on him, same thing all over again. Ten minutes. And the mask and pump, again. The paramedic couldn't say it, could get sued, but the doctor will come to pronounce death. My son. Ben. You were the light in the morning. The blue eye of heaven. When you're dead, will I be a father any more?

The doctor's hand's on my arm, the other's on Elizabeth's, as if she is trying to close a chasm between us that's so wide that people are falling into it, disappearing into the boiling earth, their screams flying up as the chasm closes, burying them, the dead and the living gone now from the sweet earth. I'm so sorry. I'm so very sorry. Let's go somewhere quiet. I'd like to tell you some things that might help a little. Let's sit down a moment. Can I bring you anything, anything at all? There's . . . well, it's over there if you need it. Yes. The nurse will bring your baby in just a minute. It's important to remember there's no extrinsic cause in most of these cases: SIDS isn't the same thing as suffocating on a pillow. It's an intrinsic problem that has to do with maturity of lung tissue, airway muscles and brain centres that control respiration or it may even be due to abnormal heart rhythms, we don't really know. Thank you, nurse. We'll leave the three of you together for a while. Please ask me if you want to know anything, anything at all. I'm sorry to have to tell you this now, but there will have to be an autopsy. It will help to know. There's no one to blame. There was nothing you could have done. Nothing more that could be done here. All resuscitation attempts were taken. There were no congenital abnormalities, no signs of concurrent illness, no evidence of trauma. It was just too late. I'll be back in a little while. Can I get someone to come sit with you? Whatever you need, please ask. A social worker will come to assist you with everything. We have a chapel and pastors and rabbis, if you'd like a service or last rites . . .

When we came back from the hospital Elizabeth said they'd been interrogating us. There were, she said, all those questions. She began to wail. All that looking at his body, all those questions. She was stripping the sheets off the crib and holding them up to the light. There are no marks, she said, putting the sheet down. Did you see how smooth his sheets were, not a rumple or a ridge, tightly

216

tucked in, nothing loose, and of course no pillow, and that woman seeming to be kind with her round face and yellow hair and you know she's never lost a baby, or opened her legs wide enough to let a child through, and her looking and making her verdict, thinking I was negligent or neglectful or downright abusive and he as white and pink and perfect as a rose and not a scratch . . . And, oh, how could you answer them so calmly, how *could* you? One after the other, the whole medical history, and not a single sob or break in your voice and even now you're not angry, you're not wanting to smash the window, you're looking out into space the way you do, not really here, not with me, I'm alone in this and will always be.

Elizabeth began to shove the sheets in a black trash bag and threw in the soft blanket her sister had lovingly made of tiny blue and white squares. Mary and I had put it flat on the floor and stitched each square and it was in the trash bag now and I was afraid to say a word to disrupt her free-fall into hell. She yanked off the mattress cover, it had a layer of lamb's wool underneath . . . Oh, if she saw this, she sobbed, she'd suggest it was too thick . . . Take it out of here . . . take it to the curb . . . Yes I do know what I'm say- ing. What? Are you crazy? Let's not do anything for a while? Like what? Not breathe for a while, not eat for a while, not scream for a while? What precisely do you mean not do anything for a while? Oh, I see, we're going to get over this, are we? . . . And don't, don't look at me like that . . . Outside the window the wind was climbing up the wall and staring in at us in our disarray and perhaps, perhaps it was the wind that came in and whisked away his breath because it was cold and this happens more in the winter and to males more than females, and less to Asian babies, and why do they have to tell us more than we need to know? Will I ever forget these words: his eyes aren't sunken and his face is blue, only slightly, just the colour of the baby's on the plane to Memphis, blue and still, pieces of sky falling into cloud. Sheets of rain hitting the window pane and occasional thunder and she says, I can see myself lying in a coffin. Torrential rain is hitting the windows and it will put out the fires and one of these days things will stop burning, even beneath the ground it will go cold so the dead can rest beneath the asphalt and the bright new streets and the shopping malls will cover everything that happened here. Pray for us now and at the hour of our death, Amen.

Elizabeth's taking off her black sweater and the tee-shirt and her skirt's up around her waist and she says it was her fault because she'd not been able to keep that first baby alive. There's been no real life between us since then. She sat on the floor and looked down at her breasts which were blue and so full of milk that the dark circles were stitched down tight and the nipples stood out purple and furious in the gloom of the room's single night-light, breasts burning and streaked with blue: I didn't ask them for anything to take the milk away, she said, and no point to put it in a bottle so you could give it if he cries because he won't cry again, he has no mother, and my breasts are just too stupid to know that. She went out and closed the door behind her. Put on a fur coat and went out into the rain to be washed away. It took me twenty minutes to find her because she was standing in the entrance to a convenience store, drenched to the bone, the fur smelling of the animal that had worn it before her, and I remember how happy she was when she got that stupid dumb coat, almost ashamed of it, but wanting it and loving how it felt in the cold when we went to Vermont and she rode her bicycle. I led her by the arm and took her back. She followed me with her head down, her hair blackening her face. I put my arms about her and for a little while she cried, but it was harsh and guttural and soon her breath was gone. I took her home, drew a bath, took her clothes off and put her in it and she lay there with her hair floating like seaweed and after a while the hot water took the pebbles out of her breasts and she began to cry unbearably in a dry, nerve-wracking way that made me want to scream or shove my hand over her mouth to shut her up. I stayed with her because I was terrified that if I left she'd hold herself under the water and lie on her long dark hair till she stopped breathing.

Dearest Hannah, I was the one who wanted a child. A son. To replace me when I died. A family to make up for the dead. Perhaps two or three children, gap-fillers. Spares. Just in case. Let me tell you these things. I might not again. Elizabeth changed after the miscarriage. Before she'd been easy-going, a good companion, our first two years together were good. After we got a house together we began to work ourselves to death to pay for it. She had an edgy side that I liked. She could do crazy things, like diving off bridges in a theatrical way, and courageous things like breaking up a fight between a man and a woman: just stopped the car, got out and ripped into the guy. She took the woman to the police station and stayed on it till the report was done. I admired her. She could be sweet and funny. She was a great cook. A good friend, kind and generous. But I hadn't chosen her. She came after me and I think that creates certain dynamics between a man and a woman. It might be a primitive thing, the need a man has to go after a woman until he's captured her, and when that happens there's a different kind of commitment. I was always stalling with her, never certain of her or of myself with her. Even in our best times there was good sex but no real intimacy. I never looked in her eyes when we made love, nor her into mine. I never once watched her orgasm. We were both in our own worlds, connected bodily but disconnected everywhere else. Our life was intellectual: it was quick and clever, but often sarcastic and damn painful. We had a pretty lethal way of communicating by the end of it.

She'd been raised with serious cash, and she was generous with it. She'd done her time in Princeton and Harvard, economics, business, she knew her foreign languages and was interested in the eastern countries. She wanted to be on top of it all, cutting edge. She worked a lot harder than I did. Liked putting in the hours while I found myself tiring of it. She believed money was magic. She thought Bill Gates could change the world. She took the miscarriage personally, like it had made her deficient for the first time in her life. I couldn't help her much because I was so crushed by the loss of that baby, so unable to get up, go to work, listen at meetings, put a deal together. I'd been making plans for it, feeling excited about the future, hoping it would make things better between us. After the miscarriage it felt like she was the one who needed all the care; she was the one who was suffering more and I kinda bought that and put my own grief on hold. But in the loneliness of it I realized I'd been lonely all along.

We couldn't help each other with it. I regret that now. We moved apart as if our own pain and grief had made the other contagious. I should have asked her to marry me then. But I didn't. I had a peculiar notion that I might not be able to make a child who could survive. I think my mother felt that way about me. We just talked about marriage and did nothing until it was too late because the moment had come and gone with the miscarriage, and the next pregnancy was really not for us, it was for her. She wanted it the way she'd once wanted that first billion dollars. She'd found her clients among the really rich after the market's long sell-off in those years following the carnage. Elizabeth Lazard was the woman who took care of all those former CEOs, and third-generation heirs, and lottery winners and movie-makers. Elizabeth up all night and flying all day, raking it in, heady with success. Until the pregnancy showed. And then she was no more the mega-broker, the high-flyer: she came to a standstill. I was stunned because every morning I'd seen her out of bed at 5.30, the buzzer going and getting louder by the second. The hairdryer and the three cups of coffee and the newspapers and the blackberry and the endless yakketty-yak of money, the bullshit and lying and the seductive late-night calls and never a minute when she wasn't checking the cellphone. The market right now's trading at seven times earnings – can I take care of this for you? And then it was all over in a heartbeat: no more in the office on Wall Street by seven on the nail. All of that blown into motherhood, folded into contentment, her body becoming its own sweet thing, filling with life. I thought we'd a chance, I thought we might make it.

I need to tell you this, Hannah, I'd like you to know that I waited for you. You're the only woman I've ever wanted to marry. And if you'll have me I won't mess up another day of our lives by not being right there where you are when you need me. I let Elizabeth down. I moved away, and not just from her, from that unborn baby, too. I didn't bond with him when he was in the belly, not like the first time. But I did try to make it work better for the two of us and I liked taking care of things for her. She was at home more, working three days in the office and two at home. She softened more as the pregnancy developed and she got less scared. About this time I got burned trying to do a deal with one of your corporate glutton types who wanted to buy up all the real estate on the outskirts of Delhi – huge financial potential, everyone getting manic and upping the stakes. Things went bad and the SEC got involved. I pulled back a lot after that, started working on smaller deals, wanted to find ways of making money in a more meaningful way. We had more time together and it was peaceful. We cut back on the competitive stuff, communicated more closely, worked for the future. I stopped hating her dad. It was a bit like at the beginning of things, but I still couldn't ask her to marry me. Couldn't get the words out. It was part of the distance between us and she was too proud to push me. I took advantage of that.

If you were to leave me for any reason or if we became estranged in the way I became with Elizabeth, I wouldn't be that way. I guarantee it. There was a level of collusion between Elizabeth and me: we wouldn't say anything that might stir up a feeling that might crack the fragile surface of our superficial accord. It was all lies. You've really taught me about lies. And you've stuck with me when I've been lying, hung in with me through a time of madness. You didn't turn away, you kept walking with me, tried to help me understand myself, including all the split-off parts that I didn't want to look at. I see now how much the amnesia reflected the way I've lived my whole life: half-asleep, dissociated, hiding out from anything that might resemble real feeling. You blasted through that and wouldn't put up with the bullshit. I appreciate it – you – more than I can ever say. You saved my life when I was hellbent on losing it.

When Ben died it was over. We came back without him, we left him there. They gave us his sleeping togs in a plastic bag and the one blue sock and the woollen hat and the wristband with his name and DOB: Benjamin Altman, 9/9/2005. Ben, son of my right hand in the Hebrew. Is he still my son? If I have other children will I count him in? Will I say I have two children and one who died or just leave it at two? I want children with you. I'm not interested in the tidy two or three, I'd like a sprawl, a mess of kids, a house in the country, and rooms without computers and cellphones. I want us all to go to Germany, and to Dresden, and put it to rest.

For a while I lived with another shell-shocked woman. Elizabeth was eating her heart out bit by bit, taking small sharp bites like a rat in a cellar, keeping it going because it was the only thing that was real to her. She was reading the autopsy time and again, like a penance. If I tried to comfort her she could not be comforted . . . I was back in the vacant lot where only the wind blows and nothing touches you, where the emptiness is filled only with grief, but if you make any connection to it you'll be burned alive, so better to extinguish yourself. She was right, I was gone, fleeing the blaze of her rage, gone into my own kind of silence, leaving her abandoned behind the white door. We both knew it was done. She said it was doomed, and she liked that word. I hated it because it was so passive. We were making another ending, another death, no one was responsible, just one of those things. And it was gutless of me to let it happen. Maybe all that was needed was for me to walk up to her and push aside the past and say, Let's try this again, let's give it all our hearts and make it work. But I didn't. And I was less of a man because of it.

I can't stay, she said, can't spend another day here. I just can't. The stairs remind me, the walls, the windows, the carpets and blinds they've all become empty spaces where I used to walk with him. You, she said, *you* remind me. She became obsessed with who was holding him that night: Was it you or me? Who was holding him? Who put him down? . . . I was so tired that night, she said, hadn't slept for weeks, up at eleven, twelve, one, two, maybe my arm fell on him, maybe when I put him down he tipped . . . I can't seem to remember. I said I'd put him down. It helped for a bit. After a month in the room with the crib, refusing to speak or see anyone, not even a doctor for medication, she and I finally sat down across the kitchen table and we spoke. A lot of people sat with us, the dead and the half-dead, of which we were a small part. The two of us sat there together and I held her hands and the hands of the ghosts walking with unspoken weights around their ankles, and what can I say to them, what is my sorrow compared to theirs, my grief to the pile-up of the corpses of the century, piled heap on heap would they touch the infinite or break through? It's no more than the reach of a single heart holding its single death in the mountainous shadow of time. So she and I sat at a table facing one another and we had no words, we had annihilated each other with our pain and on her lap, though it was empty, was the small corpse of a child.

The street was quiet, only the odd cab or the sirens going off and the planes flying overhead and the rain on the windows. Who could say why Ben left us? And who can say who was holding Rudi before he was pulled into the fire? And what more do we need to know when we know everything? He sat on the bottom stair. On the floor above, the three white doors were closed again. He sat with his hands fallen between his knees and heard footsteps outside the door, the closing of one door, the opening of another. Hannah came into the hallway. It wasn't locked, she said. Here are your keys. She looked at him and moved closer, touching his shoulder, ducking her head to kiss him. Is it okay if I'm here? He moved across to make room for her and when she sat next to him, he picked up the sheaf of yellow paper and handed it to her. She took it and glanced at the words on the first page: I was the one who wanted a child . . . to replace me when I died . . . a family to make up for the dead . . . perhaps two or three . . . gap-fillers . . . spares . . . just in case . . . She looked around her and said, Let's get out of here. Let's go home.

ACKNOWLEDGEMENTS

My thanks to Leita Hamill, Betsy Lerner, Hannah Griffiths and Sam Hynes for their contributions to the manuscript. Thank you also to Tom, my son, for all the discussions on psychopathology and my appreciation to Alexandra Martin for her help in medical matters. Love and gratitude to my sister, Angela, for her constant love and support.